The Princesses of Silicon Valley

Book 2

Nate

By

Anita Claire

NATE

First edition. November 1, 2014.

ISBN: 979-8230133834

Written by Anita Claire.

Table of Contents

Other Books by Anita Claire

Books in "The Reunion" series
Three contemporary romances stories that take place at a twenty-year high school reunion

Abby and Quinn
Kate and Noah
Harper and Liam

Books in "A Silicon Valley Prince" series
Three contemporary romance stories about adults in their 30's.

The Story of Jax and Payton
The Story of Brody and Ana
The Story of Flint and Lexi

Books in "The Princess of Silicon Valley" series
A collection of eight, coming of age, romance stories.

The Juliette Chronicles
Book 1 – Juliette
Book 2 – Nate
Book 3 – Hita

Best Friends Trilogy
Book 1 – Jennifer and Rocket
Book 2 – Isabelle
Book 3 – Kelly

Sisters from Another Mother
Book 1 – Olivia
Book 2– Meredith and Sam

Chapter 1 – High School

I t's 5:30 in the morning, about twenty-five degrees outside, and pitch black. Before I can drive my car—actually my mom's old navy-blue Volvo station wagon—I need to let it warm up. I use this time to shave the snow and ice off my windshield. Mindlessly munching on a granola bar, I listen to the crunch of the snow under my tires as I head to get my buddy, Matt. With one light honk, Matt emerges from his side door. He throws his bag in back then kicks off the snow from his boots as he slouches into my passenger seat.

"Morning Nate," he mumbles as he turns on my radio.

We drive the three miles to the Pepsi Center in silence as we listen to Santana's "Smooth" on the radio. Matt and I currently play on our town's Midget Major AAA hockey team. Our buddy Chris just moved to Canada to play AAA. Chris lives with a Canadian family as he aspires to become a professional hockey player. My parents refused to consider letting me enter the Canadian system. They're focused on me finishing high school with good grades so I can get into a top college. My dad tells me I should use hockey as a college differentiator, not a career.

I'm a good student, I study hard, but there's nothing I love more than being on the ice. Once the ref's whistle blows my world narrows down. It's just me and the eleven other guys. Pain, exhaustion, school, girls—nothing but the game is in my head. During a game, I live for the sixty minutes of play. I love tuning out the world as I relentlessly seek the puck or the guy who has the puck. The best rush ever is racing after some guy and taking him out. My hockey coach considers me his number one enforcer. I'm a big guy, relentless, I have no fear, and I'm anything but a hot head.

By the time I'm home, the lights are on and my parents are up. I cruise to my room, shower, toss on my favorite jeans and a T—the one my mom hates because it's black and the design makes me look *bad*. By now I'm starving. I'm always hungry, even when I'm sleeping I dream about food. When I get downstairs Mom has four slices of bread in the toaster. I grab a big bowl and fill it up with half a box of corn flakes. I'm hoping this, and the toast gets me through to the third period.

"Nate, don't think for a second you can leave your smelly hockey bag in the back hall. Move it now," Mom barks out, when I've only gotten to eat a full mouth full.

I pick up my bag and haul it down to the basement. Back at my seat, I pull out *On the Road*—the latest book assigned for AP English—I read while mindlessly shoveling food down my throat. Why they have me wasting my time reading about this loser is beyond me. I'm sure reading a stream of consciousness essays, about some guy traveling around America, doing drugs and listening to jazz music, was novel back in the 1950s. Today it seems like a boring episode of the *Amazing Race*. My AP Chemistry class is much more relevant and interesting.

Mom sets down a plate with a stack of toast and a jar of peanut butter as Dad walks into the kitchen. He drinks down a glass of orange juice that was waiting for him, and grabs a bagel to go, as he heads for the door.

"Son, is your game tonight at home or away?"

"The game tonight is in Tonawanda at nine," Mom replies.

"It's seven thirty, Jamie get your butt down here. I'm heading to school in five minutes. If you're not in the car, I'm leaving without you," I yell up the stairs to my sister.

Jamie comes clamoring down the stairs all in a huff, with the back of her hair still wet. She looks for her homework through the pile of papers on the chair. I grab my coat, pick up my backpack, and head for the door.

"Nate, give me another minute," Jamie whines as my mother joins her for the search.

While the car warms up, Jamie comes flying out the front door, bagel in hand.

"Will you stop at Starbucks so I can get a latté?" Jamie pleads.

"Go to Starbucks on your own time," I respond. "I'm meeting my friends before class; I don't have time to feed your caffeine addiction."

• • • •

ON THE WAY TO SCHOOL, we stop at my buddy Dan's house. Once we arrive at school Dan and I head to the table in the cafeteria my friends and I have staked out as our own. I played football in the fall and most of my friends are from the team. Once we join them, I lean back in my chair and laugh as some of the guys goof on each other. Sara and Stephanie, two hot girls from our class walk by, eliciting a number of looks from the guys.

All year long Dan has had a thing for Sara. She's tall and thin, with long legs and perfectly sculpted blond hair, but no boobs; a deal crusher for me. Whereas Stephanie is more my type, she's cute, curvy, with dark hair, and big boobs. They both smile and fling their hair as they pass by.

"Ask her out. I hear she broke up with the guy she was dating," I urge Dan.

Dan's studying Sara's ass as he contemplates my comment.

"I'll ask her out, if you ask out Stephanie," he negotiates.

"Between hockey and four AP classes, I don't have enough time to sleep. Stephanie looks high maintenance. I'm more in the market for a hookup than a girlfriend. I don't have time for all the crazy girlfriend stuff."

"Yeah, but with a girlfriend, you can get some regularly." To illustrate, he pumps his hand like he's jacking off.

"Ask her out," I prod.

The bell rings, I head to my locker, stuffing my jacket inside. Some plain looking freshman whose locker is two from mine, gives me a coy smile.

"Hi, Nate," she flirts.

"Hey," I politely respond.

AP History is my first class. Ryan, my best friend in AP, sits in front of me. With the tip of my pencil, I poke him. He maintains eye contact with our teacher as he reaches his hand up to his ear and gives me the finger.

"Dick wad, what's your problem?" he grumbles as we leave class.

"What, I thought you were falling asleep."

"Man, I can't afford to fall asleep. Colleges look at your junior grades. If mine falls off, my parents will have my balls. Are you studying after school today?"

"Running first, then I need to write my Language Arts paper before my game tonight."

"What time are you playing?"

"Not till nine. I'm already sleep deprived, and its only Monday morning."

• • • •

ON SATURDAY NIGHT WITH my backpack in hand, I enter the kitchen. "I'm taking off to Matt's for the night," I announce.

"Please be home by noon. You have too much to do to hang out playing computer games at Matt's house all day," Mom reminds me.

Dad pulls out twenty dollars, "You boys heading out for pizza and wings?"

"Keep your money. I still have plenty from last summer."

Last summer I had a cool gig working at a lab over at UB Medical School. My dad runs the ENT program at Buffalo General, where he trains all the new docs. He's considered an adjunct professor and has a lot of friends at the medical school. Between my top grades in AP Biology and my dad's connections, I got a job typically open only to college kids. The bonus of the job was Taylor Nicolson—a pre-med student at U. of R. Taylor asked me what school I went to. When I said Amherst, the name of my high school, she thought I was referring to the college in Massachusetts. Taylor's a cute nineteen-year-old, with a good rack. She spent the first week flirting with me and we spent the rest of the summer having sex at her apartment. She never did learn that I was only sixteen.

Matt, Dan, and I grab some pizza and wings, then head out to a party. When Sara and Stephanie show up, I grab Dan and march him to them. As I get Dan talking to Sara, I'm unable to control myself from flirting with Stephanie. Her lush red lips and big boobs, mesmerize me. A couple of beers have made me forget all the reasons I don't need to get involved with this girl. It takes about one beer for me to convince Stephanie to check out the back room. All too soon I have my tongue down her throat and my hands on her ass.

"I want to ask out Sara," Dan confides the next day. "Dude, do you think we can make it a double date?"

"Dan, Stephanie was fine to make out with at a party, but I really have no interest in more than that."

Dan knows my weaknesses and arranges to get us Sabers' tickets. Unfortunately, knowing I should decline *and declining* are two different things.

Now Stephanie thinks there's more going on between us then there is. It's obvious both girls are psyched, I'm wondering how I got into this mess. We head downtown early so we can get an Italian dinner at Chef's. On our drive to the First Niagara Center, my car hits a couple of big potholes, and both of my front hubcaps come flying off my wheels. We all watch in shock as my hubcaps spin on ahead of us, like they're on some ghost car. I pray that no one gets hit with a fifty-mile-an-hour hubcap. We follow them for about two blocks. Finally, they each start losing momentum and veer off to either side of the road. Quickly I park; Dan and I simultaneously catch each other's eye and blast out of the car. It takes longer than you'd think to find them, but we do.

At the First Niagara Center, we park and head to our seats. The puck drops and I'm enthralled. Stephanie cuddles up to my side and holds out her hand, "I just got a manicure, 'Flirtatious Pink.' What do you think?"

"What?"

"My nails," she giggles as she wiggles her fingers, "Didn't she do a great job? They match my lipstick." I turn as she flutters her fingers in front of her lips.

"You gonna watch the game?" I implore as I point to the ice.

She frowns and rubs her head on my arm. "I even got a pedicure."

"Do you need me to explain what's happening?" I suggest as I point to the ice.

"Last week my nail color was 'Mysterious Red.' Doesn't the name sound sexy?"

My eyes flash back to the ice in time to watch our guys as they make a great play that ends in a goal.

"YES!" I cheer and jump up, pumping my fists.

"Can you believe that guy?" I exclaim excitedly to Dan.

"Did you see how he got around both defensemen and deeked the goalie?" Dan replies.

"It was amazing." I reach over Stephanie so Dan and I can high five each other.

For the rest of the period, Stephanie sits back in her seat with a scowl on her face, while I lean forward with my arms on my legs.

By the end of the evening, it's apparent this is my first and last date with Stephanie. Without thinking it through, I drop Sara off, then Dan. As I pull into Stephanie's driveway, I realize this isn't the best plan. I should get away as fast as possible. But as I turn to say goodbye, she looks at me through her eyelashes and bites her bottom lip.

Instantly my primordial lizard brain emerges, all ego is gone only ID remains. My body becomes possessed. Somehow the car is in park, the lights are off and I'm leaning over the console. My eyes target on those pink lips. My fingers weave through her hair. She smells wonderful, she tastes even better. It's all soft lips and smooth tongues as my dick twitches from excitement. My fingers unzip her jacket as they zone in on her rack. As our kissing heats up, I somehow manage to twist my hands through layers of clothes, until I find a soft warm boob. When I knead her tit, she runs her hands over me. Everything feels so good. My mind moves to that condom in my wallet. Things can get even better.

Lights flash.

We instantly pull apart.

Her house looks like a pinball machine. All the outdoor lights are flashing on and off.

"My dad," Stephanie whispers.

"Will he leave the house?"

"He's probably getting on his boots. You better go."

• • • •

THE NEXT DAY AT SCHOOL, Stephanie comes up to me at my locker all smiley and friendly. She pops up on her tippy toes and kisses me. I stand there in shock. Oh shit, she thinks we're dating.

"**D**ickhead, you coming downstairs to the party?" my college roommate says when he throws my dirty shirt at me.

"Shit, what time is it?" I look up from my books. "Man, I've got to put in some more hours."

I'm now in my second year at Northwestern. Normally that would make me a sophomore, but since I'm in their six-year undergrad-medical school program, I'm technically considered a senior. There are pros and cons to the program I'm in. I like that I don't have to apply to medical school and it only takes six years instead of eight to get my MD. But the work is intense, only to get more intense next year when I matriculate to medical school. On top of all my class work, I'm playing hockey, and I'm in a fraternity. It's a sports fraternity and most of the guys have tutors to make it through the most basic majors. A few of us hockey players and most of the swimmers are dealing with an academically rigorous program. Next year, when I move to the Medical School located at our Chicago campus, I'll need to give up hockey. It was a hard decision to make when I chose this program. Hockey's such an important part of my life.

"Nine p.m.," Mike answers. "The girls are starting to show up."

"Yeah, I'll be down in a bit."

Enjoying a party as much as the rest of the guys, I give myself another hour to study before I brush my teeth, grab some condoms, and head downstairs.

The party's in full swing when I enter our main room. The music is loud; the drinks are flowing, while the girls are dancing. Immediately I head to the keg. One of my buddies hands me a shot of Jack.

"Nate, you need to catch up."

Doing a round of shots with my brothers, I start scoping out the crowd. I'm getting good at picking out the right girls, that is—the right girls for me. My reputation on the ice as an enforcer gives me enough of a bad boy reputation to make the girls interested. It also doesn't hurt that I'm jacked from all the training.

Immediately I zero in on a couple of potential girls. I like them curvy, dark-haired, and drunk enough to want a hookup. I never bring them back to my room. My plan is to either find some corner and screw them against the wall, use a bathroom, or if I'm lucky, they'll take me back to their place. That way I'm free to leave after we're done. College is so much better than high school.

After a beer chaser, I take a slow walk around the room; fist bumping my buddies as I zero in on tonight's girl, a hot brunette with great curves, who's showing off her rack. She gives me great eye contact and a wonderful smile. I can tell she's up for some action. Smiling back, I give her eye contact as I head to where she's dancing. It took me no time to learn that the quickest way to a hookup is honest flattery. I find the girl's one superior trait and use it in my line.

In my most casual way, I lean into her. "Hey," I murmur into her ear, "I couldn't miss you out here tonight. You have the most amazing smile."

My tight black T shows off the contours of my well-toned body. I can see the magic's already working. She smiles as she runs her hands over my biceps.

"Wow, you really work out," she purrs.

"I'm Nate," I growl.

She replies by dancing around me in a circle, showing off her nice ass. When she turns back around she gets up on her tip toes.

"Samantha," she purrs into my ear.

Not that I care about her name. I've learned when we're in bed to call them all babe.

We dance close, a couple of her girlfriend's check me out and give her the thumbs up. You don't show up at a sports fraternity party unless you want to sleep with an athlete. It's always a bit of barrel shooting to pick up a girl at one of our parties.

Samantha dances close as she tries to turn me on, which is working.

When the music stops she leans in and rubs her hand over my peck. "What sport do you play?" she questions.

The girls always know the football and basketball players. It kind of pisses me off she doesn't know who I am. I cup my hand against her ear.

"Hockey," I declare.

"Oh, Nate Lombard," she exclaims.

Cool, she knows who I am, I guess I was wrong. She must not recognize me without all the pads and helmet.

"Are you as much of a badass off the ice as you are on the ice?" she flirts.

Nodding slowly as a reply, this is barrel shooting at its finest. I make a decision, one more dance, before we leave the floor for a drink...and to move to the fun stuff.

• • • •

THE WEATHER OUTSIDE is frigid, I pull Samantha close. I'm probably not giving her any body warmth, but at least, I can block some of the wind. We finally make it to her dorm; of course, it's not as close as she made it out to be. A mile in cold weather can kill the libido. In the stairwell of her building I unzip my jacket, rub her tight against me and kiss her again, hard, this gets my juices stirring. She grabs my hand and excitedly pulls me up the three flights to her floor. Luckily, there aren't too many people hanging around, I really hate being checked out by sober people when I'm on my way to a hookup.

Completely focused, I watch as she opens her door and places a red hair thing on the outside doorknob. The lock clicks loudly as I walk past her into her dorm room. Slowly I turn around; she's leaning against the door. She's got a big flirty smile. All my focus is on her as I lean in, turn the lights on, and block her against the door. To get myself going, I take a nibble of her neck. Her skin is warm and she smells sweet. She moans deeply, the sound goes directly to my dick. My lips move along her soft skin until our lips meet. My hands search out all that warm soft skin. She rubs her groin against mine and lets out this sexy little gasp. My tongue licks against hers as my dick twitches.

"Don't you want the lights off?" She murmurs against my mouth.

"Babe, you're hot, I don't want to miss a minute of your body,"

I shed my coat and unlace my boots. With a big smile, she drops her coat. Slowly I back up as I watch her undress for me. She has a rocking body. Since she's pulling off her clothes, I start pulling off my clothes too, making sure to grab a couple of condoms out of my back pocket. My eyes are paralyzed by her perfect tits and my next favorite spot, the arc from rib cage to hip. Girls' curves drive me wild. With laser focus on her body, I get close. The heat off her body is enticing. I lean in to get my fingers and lips on her skin. She grasps me tightly and jumps up, wrapping her legs around my waist.

"Which bed is yours?" I mumble between kisses.

She points to the left. Still holding her, I brush her quilt back with one hand as I lean us down into the mattress. I drop the condoms onto the bedside table, so I can easily find them when I need them. My fingers fly over all her warm, wonderful curves, and soft smooth skin. We continue to kiss. I'm rock hard but want a taste of her tits before I come. Angling down, I get one tit in my mouth while I fondle the other one. It's amazing what I've learned in college, she must be at least a C. She moans and arches her back, which turns me on even more. I run my fingers along her wet folds until I find the warm place where I can stick a finger inside. I've learned to play around down there. As I locate the bead of her clit, I thank the Internet for providing such detailed information on how to get a girl off. She gasps and moans as I play with her nub. With my mouth on her tit, I reach for one of my condoms. I suck her tit hard, let go, blow on it. She grabs a hold of my hair and starts gasping. You'd think this would hurt, but it feels amazing. I roll on the condom as I position myself over her. Not wanting to get into the wrong kind of trouble, I make sure this is cool.

"Babe, you want this, right?"

"Yes, Nate, yes," she replies between gasps.

I smile, that's what I want to hear. She feels warm and tight against my cock. I buck into her warmth until the rhythm gets furious. She's moaning and shaking a lot so I figure she's must be enjoying this. Finally losing all control I come inside her.

• • • •

WHEN I GET BACK TO my house, the party is winding down. A few of the guys are working on a coyote; I have no idea why they don't find a nice fresh girl earlier in the evening. A buddy of mine shakes his head as I pass him. He gives me a high five.

"Dude you're a total dog."

He's probably right. But I never promise the girls I screw anything and come on; no girl can be so stupid to think they're going to find a relationship by hooking up with some guy they met an hour ago. We both know all we want are a couple of hours of no string attached sex.

• • • •

AT THE GYM, A COUPLE of the guys are showing off their new tattoos. In High School, I thought tattoos were lame. Something a dumb ass would get. College has changed my attitude. Skin art is amazing, well some of it is. One of the guys is working on a sleeve to chest, a number of guys have something on their chest, ankle, and back. Considering my chosen career, I know I need to get something that doesn't show with normal clothes. Not too many people will feel comfortable in the hands of some tatted up doctor.

I decide on an intricate Celtic knot. On my first appointment, I discuss my choice with the artist. When I go back for the actual work, I can feel the excitement or fear, I'm not quite sure which, coursing through my body.

After signing some papers, I'm lead back to the tattoo room. Surprisingly, the room looks like I'm at the dentists. There's a black leather chair that looks like it goes one hundred and eighty degrees, a wheelie chair, and a built-in counter with cabinets above and below. Everything is very clean and smells of antiseptic. On the wall are some framed intricate designs and a diploma from SAIC, School of the Art Institute of Chicago. This guy's a pro.

The artist, Kevin, enters.

"Take off your shirt," he instructs as he pulls my design out of his portfolio.

His modifications are already on transfer paper. We talk about placement. He pulls on rubber gloves, takes out a razor and shaves my arm, then applies antiseptic. Next, he sets the transfer, making sure the location is exactly where I want it. Breathing slowly and deeply I prepare myself for the work. It hurts at first. After a few minutes, it's surprisingly not that bad.

"What do you do?" Kevin asks.

He's jacked, so I know he's talking about my workout. We proceed to have a cool conversation about lifting. After Kevin finishes, he takes a picture, rubs some ointment over the art, finally he bandages me up.

That night, when I take off the bandages, I'm totally jazzed. It looks better than I ever imagined. Now I know why people get so many tattoos. I start planning my next one. Maybe I'll extend this tattoo over my shoulder and around my pec.

Medical School is a big change from undergraduate school. I'm now living in downtown Chicago, sharing a two-bedroom apartment with Dave—a friend from my undergraduate program. We're living in a modern high-rise, about four blocks from the school. Initially, the biggest change is the meal plan, there isn't one; Dave and I are responsible for cooking. We're not complete idiots but having to shop and cook takes a lot of time. We're learning to eat what's fast, cheap, and easy, which is frozen pizza, pasta, sandwiches, and cereal. One big lesson I learn, angel hair pasta cooks the fastest. I can have a hot dinner in less than ten minutes, by boiling up pasta and microwaving sauce.

Our building has a workout-weight room, pool, and hot tub, which is great since I can take the elevator down to workout at any time of day or night. Dave is not much of an athlete. I've been pulling him into the workout room, getting him on the elliptical, and lifting. On one of our early forays, as I do a series of chin-ups, I catch a hot, bottle blond who looks to be about ten years older than me, watching. Before I move to my next set, I give her good eye contact and a bit of a smirk.

She gets real close and watches me with the kettle ball. "You're in great shape," she coos.

This so could be fun. "You too look like you work out, often," I flirt back.

She extends her hand. "I'm Amy, 1407, I sell SOA services to Fortune 500 companies."

This must be the real-world equivalent of what's your major. Shaking her hand, I watch as her pupils dilate.

"Nate, 714, med student."

"Med student, I bet your patients will love you."

"I'll need to get out of med school before I find out."

"Well Nate who lives in apartment 714, I have plans for tonight. But on Thursday, how about I invite you over for dinner?"

"1407 at ..."

"Seven thirty."

In the elevator, Dave looks me over. "How did you do that?"

"Live and learn."

· · · ·

INSTEAD OF WORKING out, on Thursday afternoon I study. At seven thirty I show up at Amy's place. Even through the door, I can smell she's cooking something amazing. She opens the door and ushers me in. What's surprising is the table's all set with a tablecloth and wine glasses.

"I hope you like meat," Amy coos as she wiggles her ass and leans over to open the oven.

"Yes, I'm a red-blooded meat eater."

She laughs brightly. "Open that bottle of wine and dinner will be served in a couple of minutes."

Unfortunately, Amy spends most of the dinner talking about her job and telling me how much she hates her boss.

"More wine?" I offer to fill her glass up.

If she drinks, will she shut up so we can move to the bedroom? I inhale my steak while it takes her forever to finish. Finally, she's done. I lean over the table and clink her glass.

"How about I help you clean up?"

"Aren't you sweet."

With my plate in my hands, I follow her into the kitchen. I set my plate on the counter and lean into her, placing my fingers on her hips as I kiss that spot where her neck meets her shoulder. She leans back, melting into me. My hands run up her tummy and over her rack while my lips run a line of kisses up her jaw, ending with a nibble on her ear lobe. She lets out a long moan. My dick twitches awake.

"Where's your bedroom?" I mumble.

She giggles and clasps my hand, leading me into a room that looks like a swirl of gauzy feminine splendor. It would make me puke to live in a room like this but to fuck, hell yeah.

With an air of authority, she looks me up and down.

"Get naked," she commands.

Damn, she doesn't have to say that twice. After stripping fast, she walks around me as if she's an inspector.

"Do you like what you see?" I question.

"In my bedroom, I rule. You can only talk if I allow it," she instructs.

This is something new. I've heard about dominatrices. I'm so excited my dick jumps to attention and I almost lose it. Amy runs her fingers over my chest and down my abs. Her touch burns me with anticipation.

"You are beautiful, I can count every muscle," she coos.

She runs her finger along my dick. I suck in air as I try not to blow. She barks out a laugh and leans in.

"My Adonis do you want to fuck?"

"Hell yeah."

She walks behind me and slaps my ass, hard. Now this is freaky, but I'm going with it, as I wonder what's next. She walks around me again, trailing her finger along my torsos. She stops in front of me and licks my peck.

"Pull back my cover and get in my bed," she orders.

I scrabble for her bed in anticipation, wondering what'll be next.

She turns on some Middle Eastern music and starts dancing, while at the same time slowly peeling off her clothes. It's really hot to watch, not that I needed any coaxing; I'm doing everything I can not to blow my load.

Amy ends her dance at the foot of her bed looking down at my prone and naked body. Slowly she gets on the bed and crawls over me.

By this time my balls are so blue, I'm starting to see double. I reach up to touch her.

"You can only touch me if I tell you to," she commands.

My fingers grasp the sheets as I smile and nod in anticipation.

She grabs a hold of my dick and runs it along her folds. I gasp really loudly as her smile turns devious. From nowhere she pulls out a condom and unravels it over my dick. Then she impales herself on me, bucking hard and fast.

"Ride 'em cowboy," she yells.

If I wasn't ready to blow I would burst out laughing. She continues to ride me as she slaps my flank. It's a wild kind of pain and pleasure, that doesn't last too long since I can't hold it back.

"No, not yet," Amy whines as my dick starts to shrink.

I'm not sure what to say. But I think if she gives me a few more minutes, I'll be good for another round or two.

After giving three even freakier rides to Amy, she finally rolls over and points to the door.

"I'm sleepy, you should let yourself out," she commands.

I get back to my apartment exhausted. The next morning, as I'm chowing down on cereal, Dave joins me.

"How did your date go?"

"It was a freak show," I respond. Then unable to contain myself, I give him a few highlights of what went down.

"Are you two now a thing?"

"Amy and me? Dude, that was a pure freak show. When I left, she asked me if I was into bondage."

"Some people like that shit."

"Don't get me wrong, I like sex, but Amy. Dude, I don't want the police to find me tied to her bed."

The thing is, Amy now thinks we've shared something special and has become my own personal stalker. I'm trying to be cool about it, but in the future, I probably should avoid women in the same apartment building.

Back when we were undergraduates, I never partied with Dave. Now he's starting to learn my M.O. He watches as I casually blow off a past hookup when we run into her at the bar.

"Why did you go to her apartment in the first place if you didn't want to be with her?" Dave questions.

"Don't you want to be with a woman, but not have to deal with a woman?"

"I figured it's a total package. If you want to be with one you also need to deal with one."

"I don't have time for all the crazy stuff."

"Then choose one that you like, one that doesn't make you crazy."

"Yeah, I think my way works best. I'm way too busy to deal with a girlfriend."

"I'd rather be a lot choosier and find someone who I enjoy hanging out with. Haven't you met a woman you want to be with for more than the night?"

This conversation is moving into the feelings category. Something I don't do. Dave's a lot more serious than me, which makes me miss my fraternity buddies...and hockey.

I'm too young for any of the men's hockey leagues. To find a substitute for the physical contact and thrill of playing, I start going to a local Mixed Martial Arts studio. I need the competition, strategy, and one-on-one matchup of strength and speed that hockey gave me. MMA might not replace hockey, but it sure fits my need for that level of physical and athletic contact.

• • • •

DAVE AND I ARE A COUPLE of twenty-year-olds, whereas most of the other students in our program are three to four years older. Most medical students are serious; it's a vocation that attracts contemplative, conscientious people. Dave has a big crush on a fellow classmate, Melissa. She's twenty-three, strawberry blond hair, with a strong Texas twang. She treats Dave like a little brother, but this doesn't seem to deter him as he fights to get her to join our study group. By February, Dave's persistence has paid off as he and Melissa are now officially a couple.

At the end of the week, a group of us head to a bar to cut loose. After an hour of talking and joking, I check out the women and choose tonight's catch. I chat her up. Before we take off, I go back to our table to grab my coat.

"Nate, heading home already. The night's still young," Melissa sarcastically teases.

I give the hot brunette, who's smiling at me from the bar, a wink.

"She lives close by," I explain.

"That's your criteria?"

"What? I don't own a car. It's a pain to wait for the L at three in the morning."

"When you finally meet the right woman, you're going to fall hard."

"I can't see that happening."

• • • •

BY OUR SECOND YEAR, I have two roommates—Melissa's moved in. My rent goes down since it's now a three-way split. Melissa requires us all to chip in for a housekeeper. Which is a great improvement over our standard of living since Dave and I never cleaned the apartment. The only time dishes got washed was when we ran out, same for clothes. We don't own a vacuum cleaner, and the first time my bathroom was cleaned was when the housekeeper did it.

Melissa is great to live with. She and Dave have their issues, but they're not my issues, so I don't care. We've been branching out on our culinary choices. There's only so many frozen pizzas and boiled pasta anyone can eat. I'm now an expert at cooking chicken about a hundred different ways.

• • • •

CHRIS, MY BUDDY FROM high school—the guy who moved to Canada to play hockey—has finally made it to the majors. He'll be in Chicago when his team plays the Black Hawks. He even manages to get me a couple of tickets, and we make plans to get together after the game. After the game, my college roommate Mike and I meet up with Chris in a bar. Chris has his arms around two hot women. This makes me wonder about the road not traveled. Only five years ago, Chris and I had similar talent and skill. He's now a professional athlete. My medical career will just be getting starting when he's retiring from hockey.

• • • •

AFTER GRADUATION, I fly down to Texas to be the best man at Dave and Melissa's wedding. At the rehearsal dinner, when I'm chatting up her girlfriends, Melissa throws her arms around my shoulder.

"This is Nate, he's adorable, charming, and one of my best friends. But in the three years we lived together, he never slept with the same woman twice. If you succumb to his charms, don't say I didn't warn you."

"After living with me for three, almost four years, you and Dave won't know how to make it on your own without me," I chide her back.

"For some reason, I don't think I'll miss hearing you coming home at three in the morning."

Chapter 4 – Residence

I decide to go into orthopedics, scoring a residency at the Mayo Clinic in Rochester, Minnesota. The entire city of Rochester has a smaller population than the town of Amherst, the suburb of Buffalo where I grew up. After four years of living in downtown Chicago, living in a small company town is a big change. It hits home quickly, after I hook up with a woman at a bar, then run into her at the hospital.

On a good note, it's great to get paid instead of paying tuition. Also, for less than I was paying for a third of a two-bedroom apartment in Chicago, I now have my own two-bedroom apartment in Rochester. I buy my first car, a used blue Jeep Wrangler. At twenty-four I finally feel like I'm an adult.

● ● ● ●

MY SECOND YEAR IN ROCHESTER I start my rotation in adult reconstruction. After surgery, I head down to physical therapy to see how one of my patients is doing. I become absorbed watching him being pushed really hard by his physical therapist. She has large flashing eyes, a great smile, and a hot curvy body, but what blows me over is her personality. It's warm, tough, and focused.

"Oh, Mr. Philips, let me see you do that again," she gushes with some kind of Latin accent. She looks and sounds like a younger version of Sofia Vergara. "Wonderful," she gasps as she pushes difficult and cranky Mr. Philips to do one more exceedingly painful movement. "Here, let's see if you can do it with your foot in this position. Oh, Mr. Philips, you're a star," she cheers.

It's her amazing energy and charisma that makes Mr. Philips beam from all the attention and positive reinforcement he's getting. As the orderly wheels Mr. Philips away, the physical therapist smiles and warmly waves to him.

"I'll see you tomorrow; you'll show me all your improvements," she coos.

She turns her eyes to me. Coming close, she reads my tag.

"Dr. Nate Lombard, what can I do for you?"

"I was on the reconstruction service. I came down to see how he was doing."

"It's hard, it's painful, but we're getting him moving."

I check out her tag before flirting.

"Mariana Castro, you have a way with patients."

"He's a nice man, we all work a little harder when we're in the spotlight."

"Really, I found him to be kind of cranky."

Everyone is cranky when they're in pain. You need to look past the pain and see the person. Most people want to feel better. We get him moving and he'll get happy."

I nod and watch her greet her next patient. With her arms outstretched she smiles. "Mrs. Warner, I watched that show you recommended. Oh, you were so right. It was funny." She wheels Mrs. Warner to one of the tables. "Let's see how you're doing." As she gets her on a plinth and performs a painful stretch, Mariana's warm banter works magic on the patient. Mariana turns towards me and winks.

It's like a shot of adrenalin to my dick.

I'm stung.

I watch for the next five minutes, mesmerized by this woman.

What's going on?

When I finally manage to walk away, I can hear her warm, friendly voice in my head. I never got why guys get so stupid around women, until now. Mariana's vitality is amazing, I'm hooked. She's the human equivalent of heroin. After this one brief sample, I crave more.

• • • •

I FIND EVERY EXCUSE to head down to physical therapy...I want her...Bad.

In a small town like Rochester, my hookup reputation is now biting me in the butt.

"Oh, Dr. Nate," she banters in her amazing voice. "You're so cute, but meu amigo, I'm not going to be another one of your women."

When I find myself in physical therapy, which is more often than necessary but not often enough, Mariana always has a smile on her face, and a warm caring comment on her lips – for her patients.

But for me...

Does she know what she does to me?

Does she care?

Her melodic voice and the fluidity of her movements, make it seem like she's in a continual spontaneous song and dance. I have no idea how a woman from a tropical climate can live in Rochester, Minnesota, but I want to find out.

All the shit I gave Dave when he spent months following Melissa around happy for any bone she'd throw out, haunts me. Now I'm in the same situation.

I've started a one-man improvement course to prove to Mariana that I'm a good guy and she should date me. It's tricky since I want to be near her but don't want to get pulled in for sexual harassment.

Finding any excuse to be where Mariana is, I'm haunted with flashbacks of Amy showing up whenever I worked out. Mariana always laughs when she sees me.

"Oh Doctor Nate, you're my *cachorrinho*."

I learn that she's from Rio de Janeiro, Brazil, which helps when I look up the expression she's been using. It turns out *cachorrinho* is a little puppy.

Shit, this chick's turned me pathetic, and the worst part, I don't mind, I want more.

Out of complete desperation, I call Melissa and ask her for advice.

"This is the silliest call I've ever gotten," Melissa laughs after I fill her in on Mariana.

"Can you stop laughing and give me some advice?"

"Wait," she says chuckling. "Can I fly out and meet the woman that's gotten the notorious Nate Lombard in a spin."

"Melissa, still not helping," I exclaim annoyed, as I wonder if I should hang up now.

"Okay, Okay, Nate," she giggles. "You want to win this woman over? Then start acting like an adult. Stop hooking up. Show her by your actions that you're more than your reputation."

"Yeah, but that could take a while."

"Is she worth it?"

Damn, yes, Mariana is who I want.

Actually, it's not too hard to follow this advice since I've lost interest in going to bars to hook up. None of the women I meet have that sexy voice, big easy smile, and dismissive shrug that I'm hooked on.

After a couple of months of being Mariana's *cachorrinho* she finally throws me a bone.

"Dr. Nate," Mariana groans. "This cold weather is making me sad. I need one night of good Brazilian food and Samba dancing to get my happiness back."

Brazilian food and Samba isn't something you'll find in Rochester. Thank God for the internet, it takes me less than a minute to locate a Brazilian restaurant with Samba dancing in the suburbs of Minneapolis—an hour and a half drive from Rochester. Convincing Mariana that I'm not a crazy pervert is my next task.

"Mariana, let me drive you to Minneapolis. There's a great Brazilian place that has dancing."

"Oh Doctor Nate, this is another one of your games. I'm not that stupid."

"No games, I promise. One evening, I drive, you get to experience the warmth of home."

She sizes me up, I can feel her relenting. "Dr. Nate, don't you think I'm another one of your women."

"Never, it's dinner, dancing, and driving. Nothing else."

"I'm off on Thursday. You can pick me up at six. But none of your funny business. Clear?"

"Clear," I insist, with my most serious voice.

She heads back to her patients, as I hold my breath trying to keep myself from cheering. When I finally leave physical therapy I have the biggest smile ever.

Now I need to beg, borrow, and trade hours so I'm available on Thursday.

• • • •

EXCITEDLY I HEAD TO Mariana's. I've already made reservations and mapped out the route. Her roommate invites me in. I have a jolt of recognition. It takes me a couple heartbeats to realize it's because she works in the same ward as Mariana; thankfully it's not because we've hooked up. After waiting a half an hour for Mariana to be ready, I start questioning if she told me the correct time.

The wait is worth it…She looks amazing…Her eyes are on fire as she Samba dances down the stairs.

We bundle up against the seven degrees Minnesota temperature and head off in my Jeep. Mariana casts some Brazilian music to get us in the mood. It's the first time I've ever heard Marisa Monte, Renato Russo, or Michel Telo's music. Mariana sings along with the songs and her exuberance fills the car with joy.

The hostess seats us and Mariana bursts with excitement. "Brazilians work here. This place is authentic. I was afraid it would be owned by Americans who traveled to Brazil and now want to bring their vacation home."

Speaking Portuguese, she orders us Feijoada and Bobo. Then she orders a Malbec.

"It's from Argentina, but it's still good," she admits.

We share the food, which includes a lot of beans. As we eat, she fills me in on her choice to move to Rochester. After finishing her masters in physical therapy. After flan for dessert, we hear music coming from the back room. Mariana's face lights up as she throws up her hands and shimmies her shoulders.

"Sérgio Mendes, Dr. Nate, *vamos dançar!*"

It doesn't take a rocket scientist to realize she wants to go dancing.

I've never danced The Samba, which should make me self-conscious, but I'm so enthralled with Mariana that the thought doesn't really cross my mind. My big wish is that Samba includes some form of slow dancing, since I have a strong desire to get my hands on her body, even though I promised to be good.

"Dr. Nate put one hand on my shoulder and one on my waist," Mariana instructs.

She then proceeds to give me a personal Samba lesson. I lose track of time, but it must be over an hour that I get to touch her and hear her hum and sing to the music. The room fills up and the floor gets busy, but I only notice Mariana. At some point, she leans in.

"Dr. Nate, I need a break," she purrs, "You need to get me a *Devassa.*"

It's Brazilian beer, I order two. We lean against the bar drinking. Mariana's face glows and her smile is wide as she continues to move her hips, which is driving me wild. A few fellow Brazilian dude's come up to her. She talks to them in Portuguese as she leans into me in a flirty, possessive way. I can't help but smile as I place a hand on her waist and she shakes her butt against me. Now I know what heaven feels like.

"Dr, Nate, this was the most *maravilhoso* evening," she breathlessly affirmes on the way home. Her happiness fills my heart as she continues to elaborate, "One taste of home can help me survive this long Minnesota winter."

We pull up in front of her house as I ache to pull her into my arms. Repeatedly, I remind myself that I have to be the perfect gentleman. All I want is to hold her close, feel her lips, and get her naked. Instead, I don't even try to kiss her. I walk her up to her door and watch as she opens it.

"This was a lot of fun, we should go out again," I judiciously pronounce.

"Oh, Dr. Nate, you're so much more of a gentleman than I thought," she gushes.

Then she surprises me. She lifts up on her tiptoes and kisses me on the cheek.

Her first impression of me was correct, even so, I vow to be the gentleman she now thinks I am. I move to walk away, Mariana grabs my hand and looks at me through her eyelashes. With a sly smile she reaches again up on her tiptoes and gives me a kiss so warm and wonderful I think the Brazilian sun is now shining brightly, even though we're in the middle of a cold Minnesota night.

After what feels like forever, or maybe just a minute, she pulls away. "Dr. Nate, you're so *atraente*, now I know why the women all have problems with you."

This comment is so confusing, is this good or bad? Mariana takes one look at my perplexed expression and barks out a good laugh.

"It's cold out here." With a flirty wink her melodic voice gets husky, "Next time, I'll invite you in."

• • • •

MY ROTATION MOVES ME to the Orthopedic Trauma Service, which turns out to be good timing since I'm now caught, as they say, "hook, line, and sinker," into Mariana. I'm still trying to keep in shape—and, of course, working at the hospital, at least, sixty-five hours a week—but every available free moment is now taken up by Mariana.

She makes me hire a cleaning lady, since I'm never going to do it and she won't stay in my filthy apartment. I've also learned that she's never on time for anything, can spend an hour on her hair, changes her clothes three times before she finally decides what she wants to wear, and expects me to make dinner reservations since she doesn't like to wait in line. If I don't compliment her on how she looks or text her at least twice a day, she loses it on me. After seeing her for only a few months I think I can write a Mariana rulebook, though what's the point, no other guy is ever going to go out with her.

At least half of my day is spent in the operating room, I find that surgery gives me the same focus I get when competing in sports. When I play hockey, in MMA completions, and now in the OR, the world around me narrows, I have laser focus. My mind is targeted on the task at hand I have no idea about time or any activity outside of what I'm doing.

This has become problematic in my relationship with Mariana since she doesn't like to be left waiting around. I'm now getting really good at texting her before surgery, telling her what OR I will be in so she can find out when I get out. If I forget and show up late, there's holy hell to pay.

• • • •

WHEN MARIANA AND I both have a weekend off, we fly to New York City to visit Dave and Melissa—sleeping on an air mattress in their small Brooklyn living room.

After a fun day of taking in the sights and eating ethnic food, Melissa pulls me aside.

"I can't believe that out of all the women out there, you've chosen the highest maintenance, most demanding woman in the world," she exclaims.

"Yeah, I know, but isn't she amazing."

"What alien has taken over your brain?"

• • • •

AFTER WE'VE BEEN GOING out for six months, Mariana moves in with me. I'm glad I have a two-bedroom apartment since she moves all my things out of the bigger master bedroom closet and into the spare bedroom closet. She also fills the master bathroom with all her products.

My undergrad roommate, Mike, comes for a visit and can only shake his head.

"Nate, you're totally whipped," he jokes.

Actually, I think it's amusing since I find Mariana...captivating.

Living with Mariana is a whole new world then dating her. She has a number of bazaar Brazilian rules. Really, I have no idea if they're Brazilian rules, but she has a unique way of doing things and it's not worth an argument—I have no desire to go against the tide.

Mariana also has a propensity for losing her keys, getting lost, and forgetting to do basic things like to fill her car with gas. All of which ends in calls to me to fix the problem. Regardless, Mariana brings such joy into my life, and frankly, the sex is so hot, I'm a happy man.

• • • •

MY THIRD-YEAR ROTATION for sports and arthroscopy is in Florida and it comes in the middle of winter. Before leaving for three months, Mariana and I take a two-week vacation to meet her family in Brazil.

Mariana is not happy about me being in Jacksonville. In an attempt to make it up to her, I get in the habit of texting her first thing every morning, then follow up by calling her on the way to work, and again calling her every night on my way home.

Before I left she was having problems with her car, so I let her use my Jeep while I lease a car in Jacksonville. Also, I'm still paying my half for our apartment. None of this seems to please Mariana. She still wants me to pay for her to fly back and forth to Jacksonville every other week.

I'm already stretched after our expensive vacation, paying my share on two apartments, and leasing a car. It's hard to admit but I tell her I can't do it.

Even without Mariana, I'm enjoying Jacksonville's warm winter weather. It's nice not to have to battle the snow, and with this sports and arthroscopy rotation, I think I've found my calling. This makes me think of my future. After I finish my residency, maybe Mariana and I can move someplace warmer. After a month of being away from Mariana, I miss her so badly I bite the bullet and buy her a plane ticket to visit me on the anniversary of our first date.

Her whole trip is now on my credit card, which makes me crazy since I hate running up debt, but I figure this is an emergency. At work, I juggle my schedule around so that I work twelve days straight before and after her visit. This gives me the needed days off. I wait in anticipation to see Mariana. We spend three amazing days, mostly in bed since I can't get enough of her.

• • • •

AS I START MY THIRD year, with less than two years remaining on my residency, the real issue comes to a head. Mariana brings up marriage and kids. This whole line of thought is kind of shocking since none of her siblings are married, even though they're all living with their significant others.

All my plans include Mariana, though I don't feel ready to get engaged. My life doesn't have the time for a wedding and I can't even think about kids, even though I know at some point I'd like to be a dad. For a week, we have explosive fights, in which she's explosive and I tiptoe around hoping I don't get impaled by any of her shrapnel.

Finally, Mariana calms down enough so that we can have a reasonable conversation.

"Mariana, I love you. Your part of all my long-term plans, I just don't want to get married until I'm done with my residency."

"You don't love me enough to put a ring on my finger," she wails.

"I will in two years."

"That's what a man says if he's stringing a woman along."

It's a year earlier than what I planned, but if it will make Mariana happy, I'm all in. Biting the bullet, I ask my dad for money so I can buy an engagement ring. This is so much harder than I thought, I don't want to be leaning on my parents anymore. The thing is, I don't have any cash and after finally paying off her trip, I don't want to put something as expensive as a ring on my credit card if I can't pay it off. My parents are supportive. Mom actually comes through, sending me my grandmother's diamond engagement ring.

A couple of days after talking to my parents, I get a call from my sister Jamie.

"What absolutely shockingly stupid thing are you about to do now?" my sister's voice booms at me.

"What?" I respond in confusion.

"Mom called me and said you're asking that insane woman you live with to marry you. Please, tell me this isn't so."

"Call me when you're rational."

"You don't get to hang up on me, Nate. This is my future sister-in-law you're talking about, my future nieces and nephews. Why would you want to marry that insane woman?"

"Frankly, you're the one that sounds insane. Anyway, I love her, she makes me happy."

"Nate, she's difficult, always playing control games, and not much of a partner, besides you have nothing in common. Name one thing you do together?"

"We enjoy each other's company."

"Please don't tell me you're asking her to marry you so she stops throwing tantrums."

"Jamie, she's my future. Get used to it if you want to stay in my life."

We end the call on a difficult note. Why is Jamie being such a jerk? After that bazaar conversation, I lie in bed awake. It finally hits me, Jamie doesn't understand. I love Mariana, I want her to be happy, and I want to be with her.

· · · ·

BEFORE I HEAD OFF TO Jacksonville again, Mariana and I take a one-week vacation to the Virgin Islands. I get to swim and run on the beach every day. Mariana joins me on the boat when I scuba dive. For dinner, we go to a romantic restaurant, between courses I take her for a walk on the beach at sunset. I and go down on one knee.

"I love you; I want us to be together forever. Marry me, make me the happiest man in the world, say yes."

"Oh Nate, yes, meu amor, yes," she coos.

I pull out my grandmother's two-carat diamond ring and place it on her finger.

"I know this ring doesn't fit, but tomorrow we can go to one of the jewelry stores. You can pick out any setting you want. They say they can have the ring for us before we leave."

On our second to last day, I make a point of doing what she likes. Ordering a half-day spa session for her in the morning and visiting jewelry stores in the afternoon.

· · · ·

THE ROTATION IN JACKSONVILLE is much easier the second time since I already know the drill. After I get back to Rochester, Mariana and I enjoy a fun summer hanging with friends. All seems to be well. I come home from work late one night and see a sheet from a prescription pad on the kitchen counter. Mariana's engagement ring is on top. The note says:

Dear Nate,

I love you, but love isn't enough. I thought it would be easiest if I left quietly. I've taken a job in Atlanta. Good luck with your life.

Mariana

What?

I'm in shock.

This can't be.

We've been together for almost three years. No conversation; all I get is a Dear John letter. Why? What went wrong? What didn't I do?

I find myself walking around our apartment like a zombie cataloging my life. She's taken what she wanted and left what she didn't want, which includes me. Some of her toiletries and clothes are still in the closet and in the bathroom. Our bed, the bed I bought, is gone while her old crappy bed remains in the guest room. The couch I paid for – that she chose – is gone, while the chair she bought – that I've always hated – remains. Most of the stuff in the kitchen is gone, though she left me the fancy coffee maker she had to have. Then again, she never could figure out how to use it.

After an hour of idle wandering, I call her phone and get moved directly into voicemail. I then spend the next few days blowing up her phone with messages and texts. I start off with; *What happened?* and move to; *Why did you leave?* And end up with: *Please come home.*

At one in the morning, I'm on Facebook and Instagram, she hasn't blocked me from her page. I scroll through her history, our history. At three in the morning, I find myself down on the floor, holding the engagement ring between my thumb and finger, and cry. I think it's the first time I've cried since I was a child.

· · · ·

INEVITABLY, A FEW DAYS after she leaves, I run into one of her friends.

"Hello Nate," she uncomfortably greets me.

"Do you know if Mariana got to Atlanta safely?"

"Yeah, we've been texting. She's getting settled in."

Now I know her phone's still working. With a million questions floating through my mind, I don't know how to formulate any of them. The last thing I want to be is pathetic.

"I'll see you around," I casually add as I head to my car.

I find myself sitting in my car, paralyzed. Only work forces me to move.

I've been avoiding calls from friends and family, texting back lame excuses like; *Really busy*.

At some point, the sadness moves to anger. I've become a holy terror at MMA.

· · · ·

"WHEN WERE YOU GOING to tell me that Mariana left?" Melissa says when I answer my phone.

"How'd you hear?"

"Facebook. I saw she changed her city and relationship status. How are you doing?"

"Me, I'm fine."

"You're such a liar."

"But it's how I get through the day... Melissa, why'd she leave? She never said anything. I came home one night and she'd move out."

"I have no idea. What do her friends say?"

"Yeah, I'm going to call up her friends. We'll all sit around, paint our nails and talk about our feelings."

"Maybe she thought marrying you would make her happy. When she still wasn't happy after you guys got engaged, she had to leave."

"What does that mean?"

"That means she had this bright personality, but the woman underneath wasn't happy. She was looking for someone else to make her happy. When that didn't work, she had to move on."

"I would have been there for her."

"Yeah, but that might not have been what she wanted. Anyway, I barely knew the woman. It's you I care about."

"I'm going to be fine."

"Yeah, I know you are. I called to tell you that your friends care."

．．．．

AFTER WEEKS OF AVOIDING Jamie, I finally pick up the phone when she calls.

"You sure dodged a bullet on that one."

"Fuck you," I exclaim as all my anger rises to the surface.

"Come on, Nate, that chick was a bat shit crazy control freak. You spent almost three years catering to her every crazy ass whim. When messing with you no longer made her happy, she had to move on. "

"But, why did she sneak out? Why didn't she, at least, tell me?"

"And what would you have done if she told you?"

"Convince her to stay."

"You now have your answer."

There is a long pregnant pause.

"How's California?"

"I'm happy. I'm playing soccer, I like my job, and the weather's great. No little white line on my shoes from the snow and salt. Nate, come out here. You're almost done with your residency. When you're done, come to California. It would be great to have you nearby."

"Yeah, whatever."

"Don't, 'yeah whatever' me. There's nothing for you in Minnesota. Come to California. Hey, promise me this, at least, you'll come, stay with me and check it out."

"I've been to California plenty of times."

"No, check it out for work. We haven't lived in the same town for ten years. It would be great to have you close by."

"Okay."

"Okay you're blowing me off, or okay you'll look for jobs near me?"

"Okay, when the time comes I'll check out jobs near you."

• • • •

FOR MY LAST NINE MONTHS, I'm the chief resident. With gallows humor, I think this worked out well since Mariana would have hated the extra time chief resident requires. I'm also in great shape since I don't have much of a life other than working and working out. On my days off I head north to snowshoe or cross-country ski.

• • • •

A FEW MONTHS AFTER Mariana leaves, I head to one of the bars I went to when I was single. But I sit in my car staring at the building unable to get motivated to go inside. A few weeks later, I join a couple of guys from my hockey team as they head to a sports bar. We watch a game. My eyes linger on the women at the bar, I know exactly who I'd hit on if I wanted a hookup. But the thought of a hookup feels shockingly depressing; I have no interest in sleeping with random women. I'm finally at a point where I can say, I want another girlfriend. I'm just not ready to find one.

During my winter vacation, I go scuba diving in the Andaman Sea, staying in Coh Pee Pee, Thailand. It takes forever to get there, but I'm not ready to go back to the Caribbean, it has too many memories. On the first day of scuba diving, I meet a reserved, tall, thin, blond, German woman who's traveling alone. She's the polar opposite of Mariana. After scuba diving for the day, we go out for dinner and spend the next ten days in each other's arms. It's the first time I've been with a woman since Mariana left. Lying in bed with her, I know she's not my future, but I realize that I'm moving on, which is good.

Back in Rochester, friends try fixing me up. The women are nice, but none touches my heart. Maybe it's still too broken.

At the end of my residency, after passing my boards, I get offered an attending position at the Mayo Clinic. I also get an offer for a fellowship to the Jacksonville facility. With my sister's haranguing, I apply to a couple of sports medicine clinics in Northern California. When an interview opportunity for a fellowship in Palo Alto comes up, I fly out and stay with Jamie the weekend before.

On Sunday morning Jamie has a soccer game, I join her as a spectator. It's a good game; the teams are evenly matched. By the end of the first quarter, the other team puts in two defenders. Both are pretty, little women. At first I think it's a joke. Jamie will blast through both of them with ease. But quickly I learn, they might be petite, but they're fast, fierce, and relentless. They keep on frustrating Jamie and her teammates.

Near the end of the game, Jamie has a break away. I figure she's about to score when one of the little defenders zooms in and gets the ball away from her. The defender heads up the sidelines as Jamie and her teammate tries to get the ball back. The defender dekes around Jamie's teammate and runs smack into Jamie, as if Jamie's a wall.

The defender totem poles over and lies flat on the ground. Part of my training included being the on-field physician for the local high school's football and basketball teams. Since I'm experienced with field injuries, I head to where the little terror lays. She's not unconscious, just stunned. Since no one else seems to have a medical background I take the lead and monitor her movements.

"Can someone give me a hand up?" she murmurs.

"Are you sure you're ready to get up?" I question.

She seems to be having some problems getting her legs under herself. We must get her off the field so they can finish the game. But we need to see if she's injured. Not surprisingly, she's scrappy.

"Easy now, not so fast, give yourself some time," I coach as she tries to get up.

When she attempts to stand again, I grab her under her arms, just in time since I feel her start to go down. My goal is to make sure she doesn't fall and hurt herself. She pulls herself together, and with some support from me walks off the field.

She favors her right ankle. I spot a blanket by the other spectators. Setting her down, I quickly unlace her shoe; pull off her shin guard, and sock. I check out her ankle to make sure she didn't injure it. Slowly I work my hands up to her knee.

"Wow, wait a second, buddy, just because I might be injured doesn't mean you can feel me up," she exclaims as she tugs her leg out of my grasp.

I've been so focused on her medical needs I haven't paid attention to how pretty she is.

"I'm a doctor, orthopedics. I'm making sure you haven't injured anything."

"Seriously, you're a real doctor?"

She sure is feisty. She definitely isn't flirty. But what knocks me out is her beautiful porcelain skin flushed with exercise and these huge dark eyes. Her features are soft, feminine, and petite while her personality is fierce. It's a compelling juxtaposition.

"Seriously, I'm a medical doctor."

"What, business is slow at the hospital so you show up to women's soccer games hoping to get some action?"

"Only soccer games my kid sister's in."

"Who's your sister?"

"The player who took you out."

"What! Does she bring you for back up when she attempts to kill opposing players?"

"You're as pugnacious off the field as you are on the field."

"I don't know if I should be flattered or repulsed by that comment?"

There isn't anything wrong with this woman's leg. No guy has shown up to claim her. If she was my girlfriend, I sure would be right there if someone took her out. Maybe she's single; she sure is pretty. More than being pretty, I like her attitude. Man, this is the first woman I have felt any real interest in since Mariana left me a year ago.

To finish up my sideline exam, I pull a penlight out of my back pocket and check to make sure she doesn't have a concussion. My concentration is hijacked by her beautiful dark eyes that are really dark green. How do I ask her out without coming off smarmy?

"It doesn't look like you have a concussion and the ankle looks like it will be okay," I conclude in my most professional voice.

"Don't you need X-rays or an MRI to know if there's a problem?" she questions.

"If I thought there was a problem you might need an X-ray or an MRI," I reply.

She's not really a patient, maybe a little flirting would be okay. I weigh the implications and decide to go for it.

"I'm looking at a perfectly fine pair of legs," I concede as I give her eye contact and a small flirty smile. "It looks like you may have tweaked your ankle a little."

"How do you know that I don't have any damage to my spine?"

"How does your body feel?"

"I haven't tried to stand, but sitting here now, I feel normal."

"Why don't you try to stand?" I grab her by the arm in case she falls over.

I twitch and almost gasp as my whole arm tingles from contact. Then I step back and watch her wiggle around, I appreciate the rest of her body, it's as nicely proportioned as her legs. It's hard to tell with the baggy soccer clothes but she looks slim, curvy and stacked.

"I don't even know your name—to say thank you," she says.

"Nate, Doctor Nate Lombard," I exclaim with my best flirty smile.

"Doctor Nate Lombard thanks for helping me, I'm Juliette."

She has a pretty smile that matches her pretty face. California is looking up; maybe I should seriously consider moving here.

"Juliette, whose last name I don't know, I'm glad my little sister didn't hurt you. "

"Cole, my last name's Cole."

"Juliette Cole, I'm glad my little sister didn't hurt you."

"I'm free to go home?"

"I would take it easy for the rest of the day. Ice the ankle. It probably would be a good idea if you take an Aleve."

Our eyes connect, it feels like something good is happening...Juliette Cole...Damn.

There's this spark that flashes between us. I didn't think I'd ever feel that spark again. As I contemplate what to do next, Jamie surprises me by placing her hand on my arm. She sizes me up quickly and then looks at Juliette.

"Sorry, you're a good player," Jamie good-naturedly comments. "I was trying to get the ball away from you. I hope my brother wasn't a jerk."

"No problem. That was a fun game," Juliette replies. "Your brother was kind."

I'm about to ask for her number when the other little defending terror interrupts. Juliette turns away. Something is happening, I can feel it. I watch the two women talk. Jamie pulls on my arm. As she pulls me away, I give Juliette one last look. I have her name; how hard can it be to find someone in today's connected world?

"I was worried about you for nothing. Looks like you're back to hitting on women," Jamie comments on our walk back to her car.

It's the first day, in what feels like forever, I feel like my old self.

• • • •

BACK AT JAMIE'S, AS she showers and changes, I type, "Juliette Cole" into Google. A link to her LinkedIn, Instagram and Facebook page along with her alumni information comes up. She's pretty and smart. It looks like she graduated this past spring with a Masters in Engineering and Computer Science. This must make her around twenty-four or twenty-five. Farther down, there are a number of links to papers she's written. I've never heard of the k-means algorithms or the Apriori algorithm. I click on the papers, not surprisingly, it's filled with equations and charts with very few understandable words.

I bring up a presentation she gave at a conference; it's definitely her. She's articulate and poised. Her eyes flash dark and her face looks pale. The camera doesn't catch the luminescence of her skin. At the soccer game her hair was held back in a braid, on the video, it's long and curly. Jamie interrupts my contemplation. I close my computer and we head out to meet up with some of Jamie's friends.

The next morning, I find myself still thinking about the lovely Juliette Cole. During my first rotation in Jacksonville, I got into the habit of texting Mariana every morning. It became part of my routine, like brushing my teeth. After Mariana left, I no longer had anyone to text in the morning. The absence of that routine made me feel like I forgot something as I headed off to work.

On Facebook I find Juliette, and then message her, something professional. Hopefully, I can use this as a good opening:

Nate: *I hope no unpleasant side effects, are you feeling well today?*

Half way to my interview my phone beep's, Juliette's responded.

Juliette: *Feeling fine, I guess it was the fast medical attention. Did your sister have a problem with you saving the opposition?*

It's not flirty, but then again, she was friendly, not flirty. I wait until the next morning; I wouldn't want to come across as desperate. This time, I add a little flirt to my text.

Me: *I'm not that fast but I am thorough.*

Juliette: *Are you a thorough doctor or do you have an ankle fetish?*

That was a flirt, let's see what kind of offer I get from this practice, I might be seeing more of Juliette Cole. After a day of tours and interviews, I get a pretty good idea of how they run their practice. I'm starting to think that this might be my next job. Juliette Cole won't be the reason I'll move, but I take meeting her as a sign that Northern California should be my next destination.

The next morning, I flirt: *I have a lot of interests and my fetishes aren't limited to ankles.*

Juliette: *Name one of your interests?*

While I wait in the lobby of the medical offices, I have a smile on my face. I wonder if it's flirting, or having a woman that I want to flirt with is what's making me happy? Too bad she didn't go with fetishes, now that could have been fun. She seems like a sweet, good girl. I think I might be ready for one like that.

Me: *I like playing hockey.*

Juliette: *Is your sister as big a fan of your hockey games as you are of her soccer games?*

Clever girl. I bet she figured out I'm in Minnesota and is trying to find out more about me. I should give her a bit of help.

Me: *Hopefully she will be soon, I'm currently interviewing for a position in Palo Alto.*

It feels good to have someone to text in the morning. About a week in, I get a departure from Juliette's G-rated flirty texts.

Juliette: *My roommate's dating Luke Tomlin. She scored us tickets to today's football game.*

Now that's unexpected. I didn't take her for the type that hangs with pro-athletes. Did I read her wrong?

I'm off on Sunday. After a double workout, the MMA studio in the morning then a hockey game in the early afternoon, I join my buddies at the local sports bar. The game of the week is from San Francisco. The weather in Santa Clara looks beautiful; Juliette is in for a good game.

As they deliver my burger, I almost fall out of my seat. On TV, they flash to a gorgeous blond throwing kisses to Tomlin...and next to the hot blond is a woman that looks like Juliette. I snatch my phone and scroll to our conversation thread. She said her roommate's dating Tomlin. That was not a figment of my imagination, that has to be Juliette on TV.

As the game proceeds, I'm transfixed. Will they flash on that blond again; is it really Juliette she's with? When they showed them earlier, I was so surprised and it was for only a few seconds. Juliette looks hot, but in the couple of seconds, it took me to register the face I'm not sure if it's really her. After San Francisco wins back the ball, they flash on Tomlin's girlfriend again; Juliette is clearly in the frame, leaning with her elbows on her knees. She has that same demure, sweet smile. Although, I'm sure no one is looking at her face but me, since her tight low-cut shirt provides a perfect cleavage shot and she has an amazing rack. Is this the same woman I met last week and I've been texting? The woman on TV looks like sex on a stick.

"Lombard, wipe the drool off your chin," my buddy teases me.

"Last Sunday I met that woman when I was visiting my sister. I've been texting her all week," I exclaim as I point to the screen.

"The blond?" he asks with a face filled with shock and awe.

"No, Juliette, the brunette," I explain. Damn, those soccer clothes definitely hid a hot little body.

"Man, I've heard stories about you, but I thought it was bull," one of the guys comments.

I'm transfixed on the game, while I ponder, who is Juliette?

Before halftime, they flash on the blond and Juliette again. All the guys at my table cheer loudly. Juliette's standing with her hands over her head and her hot, curvy body is on full display in that tight top. When I go back for the partner interview, I'm determined to take her on a date.

In the second half, they flash on Juliette and her roommate three more times. They're joking in the booth about how hot Tomlin's girlfriend is. One of the broadcasters is totally smitten. Someone figures out she was in a beer commercial a few years ago. One of the guys I'm with, points to a beer poster on the wall of this bar. It's Juliette's friend. This makes me wonder, who is this Juliette?

• • • •

IN THE MORNING, AFTER spending a night fantasizing about Juliette in that top, I debate what to text her.

Me: *Great football game, did you have fun?*

My phone beeps on my way to the ER.

Juliette: *It's always fun when they win. Are you a fan?*

Usually, I wait until the next day to respond, but her hot body in that red T-shirt plagued my dreams.

Me: *Buffalo's my team—they're not doing as well as your guys.*

Juliette: *Buffalo?*

Me: *That's where I grew up.*

Juliette: *There's always next year...or you could cheer for a better team.*

Me: *blasphemy!*

Juliette: *So you pray every Sunday to the Buffalo team?*

Me: *I pray every Sunday FOR the Buffalo team.*

My attending gives me a strange look as he watches me slide my phone into my pocket.

"You sure are in a good mood," he comments.

"Life is looking up," I reply.

• • • •

THE NEXT MORNING, WHEN I go to text Juliette, I see she responded to my last text.

Juliette: *That was my first NFL game – lots of fun – need to do it again.*

If I get this job, I might be the guy taking you.

Me: *My buddies didn't believe me when I said you were the woman in California I've been texting.*

Juliette: *I had no idea Cassie and I were on national TV. I couldn't understand how everyone knew I went to the game.*

• • • •

TEXTING WITH MARIANA was easy—shit like, "*have a good day,*" or "*Charm angry patient,*" or "*I'll be in OR 5 until 3.*" Juliette and my texts are rather lame. I've never wanted to text a woman, other than Mariana. The last time I was single, texting let alone sexting, wasn't a thing. Now, I'm not even sure what to write; though this woman is hot and I'm assuming single. I know I wasn't the only guy who jacked off to images of her hot little body last Sunday night. If I don't work on keeping something going, someone else is going to jump in and steal my game.

I'm about to send Juliette my good morning message, when I realize, last night, she sent me a picture. I scroll down and let it load; it's of her hot ass. Not naked, but it's a sexy angle and not a selfie. Did one of her friends do this as a prank, or is she one of those tigers who presents as a lamb? Whatever, I'm not going to complain.

Her picture gives me an idea. Not a dick shot, I still don't get what's with that. I stand in front of the mirror and take a selfie of the tattoo on my bicep.

I crop it.

Send it

Damn, this is fun.

And a lot better than trying to think of what to say next.

Our texts continue, with interesting sexy G-rated selfies. She sends me a photo of her lips all glossy and puckered up for a kiss, I send her a picture of my back flexed.

A week later, I get a call back from the practice in Palo Alto.

As soon as I have a plane reservation, I set up a date with Juliette.

My flight gets in early, giving me plenty of time to rent a car and navigate to Juliette's place. I'm excited to see her. That low cut red shirt with her boobs in full display, is seared in my mind. Is her skin as luminescent as I remember; is she as spunky? I know she's hot. My GPS leads me to a tree-lined residential street. With a deep breath to manage my energy, I ring the doorbell. It takes a few heartbeats before I hear the lock move.

"Hey," Juliette says.

She's as pretty as I remember, wearing those yoga pants that all the women are now wearing. They show off her hot little body. Lycra is my favorite material.

"Hey," I coolly reply,

With a sweep of her hand, she invites me in. I watch as she grabs her phone and purse. Could she be ready?

"Do you want to drive or do you want me to drive?" Juliette casually asks.

"Do you know where we're going?" I reply.

"Yes, I hope so. It's not too far from here," she says.

Shit, I didn't mean to offend her, I'm just used to Mariana. Though explaining myself would be worse than letting my comment ride. Juliette points through the open door towards the hills to the west.

"We're going to the top of the mountain."

"I'll drive," I say.

Juliette competently navigates us through her town. Our conversation is stilted. With all the texting, I was hoping our first date would be easier.

"Do you do this often?" I blurt out. Then realize that sounds weird. "Hike and wine taste that is."

"Surprisingly, not that often. It's a great way to spend the day, but I guess living here I get busy with life."

Our conversation continues, we talk about school and why I'm in town. We pass a reservoir.

"We're getting close to the street we want to take. It's up there on the right," Juliette explains. "I should warn you, it's all uphill with hairpin turns, the road is narrow, and there are a lot of cyclists."

"Wait, you're taking me on a steep, narrow, twisting road with cyclists, to go wine tasting?"

"Yeah, kind of an oxymoron."

"I don't think that's the correct word," I say.

What a stupid comment. I'm way too rusty with this dating thing. Then again, I don't know if I was ever any good at it. Until Mariana, I never really tried.

"What would you call it?" Juliette responds.

"Ironic...?" I put forth.

"Ironic? Yeah, I guess that would work, or maybe juxtaposed."

That ends our conversation. Juliette gets quiet and stares out the window. I hope it's because she's one of those women that doesn't need to fill every second with conversation. I need downtime to reflect, or maybe to save myself from another stupid comment.

We continue to drive up the mountain. When we finally get to a point when I wonder if this mountain will ever end, we reach a gate.

"It's only a couple mile walk to the view," she explains as we get out of the car.

The blue sky and warm temperature feel wonderful. I shed my fleece and grab the water bottle I took on the plane. We skirt around the gate and walk down a wide dirt road past a series of communications towers. The road opens up and Juliette navigates us to an area with a number of rocks.

"To our left you can see the Pacific Ocean, to our right you can see the bay. How familiar are you with the bay area?" she questions.

"I've been here a few times—to San Francisco, Napa, and Monterey."

Juliette points out landmarks. All I'm interested in is her. She's pretty, really pretty. But, she's pretty in that way women who don't care about being pretty are. Some good looking female doctors I know are that way; they don't derive their ego from their looks. What they share is an unencumbered attitude. I like that. She was ready when I came to the door, no games. She probably doesn't change her outfit three times before she goes out either. Juliette's different than Mariana, which is good.

"What?" she asks with a questioning smile, once she realizes I'm looking at her, not the view. I shake my head. A pretty girl like her should be used to guys checking her out.

"Drink up," Juliette urges. "Because it's so dry, you don't sweat that much here. People from back east never realize how dehydrated they're getting."

I follow her recommendation, while I can't seem to keep my eyes off her. Our conversation turns easy and fun as we head back to the car on the same path we took. She directs me down the hill to the winery.

"I recommend we put something in our stomachs before wine tasting," I suggest. I grab the bag with food out of the back. "You lead the way."

There's a picnic area near the tasting room. She's chosen some nice cheeses, fresh bread and fruit. The weather feels like early September in Minnesota. The air is warm with a hint of a cool breeze, the sun feels good. While at home, the leaves are off the trees and we've already had snow flurries. When we're done eating, I gather up what's left and put the bag back in the car.

We meet back up by the door of the tasting room. My fingers itch to touch her. Casually placing a hand on her back, my whole arm tingles from contact. This is nice. I can't help but smile.

We each choose a wine series to taste and stand shoulder to shoulder at the bar. We're so close I can't help but look at her soft pink lips and wonder what they'll feel like, what sounds she'll make when she comes. With great restraint, I pull myself back, I'm not twenty, this isn't a hookup. I need to slow down. Juliette's a nice girl, the type I spent my youth avoiding. I can tell by her body language, if I push her too fast, she'll run. Then again, catching her might actually be fun.

"This one is good," I purr into her ear as I enjoy watching her eyes dilate. She reaches to take my glass, our fingers brush against each other. My skin sparks while she bites her lip. I hold my breath, to keep myself from leaning in and biting her lip too.

The more wine we taste, the more Juliette relaxes. Which is good, since it's fun to watch her flinch from excitement when I casually touch her.

"This one has an incredibly sexy nose which is followed by an expansive sumptuous texture and a long, thirty-five -second finish," our pourer explains as he shows us the next pair.

As he walks away Juliette starts to snicker. "Did he just describe the wine or his last encounter?"

"If his finish last thirty-five seconds, I don't think he should brag," I flirt.

Our eyes connect. Her mouth turns into an O as she gasps My dick twitches from the sound. Damn, she has this naive, fun, thing going. It's the best juxtaposed of the day. Every moment I'm with this woman, I want to be with her more. I can feel her sucking me in, after this last year, having this side awoken, feels exceptionally good.

Before we leave, I buy a couple bottles of the wine we both liked best, I figure I can bring one tonight to the partner dinner and leave one with Juliette. It will be a thank you for the nice day and an excuse to have dinner with her in the future.

I flash back to Mariana and our first date. I was such a gentleman. Then she pulled me into that kiss.

In front of Juliette's apartment, my eyes move to her juicy lips. I can feel all her barriers are back up. I'm an adult, no need to rush this, I've got time. Sometimes waiting can make it better.

I walk Juliette to her front door. I can feel she's holding herself close. Gone is the flirting and all the sexual innuendos. Obviously, she's not the kind of woman who does a casual hookup, which is cool. Well, not cool, I'd love to taste her skin, but I have patience, I can wait. At the door I don't try to kiss her or even touch her, I diplomatically hand her the bottle of wine.

"I enjoyed our day. Can I give you this bottle with the hope we can share it in the near future?"

"Sure, today was...nice."

I stand on her stoop and watch as she closes the door. *Juliette Cole, now this is worth pursuing.*

At my hotel room, before I take off for dinner, I shoot Juliette an e-mail.

Me: *Great day, thanks for being my guide.*

Back in Rochester, the job offer from Palo Alto comes in. My boss at Mayo knows I was planning on moving on, and he's been supportive. After five years living in the same apartment, I need to pack up, say goodbye and leave. On the Internet, I find a one-bedroom apartment with a designated parking space, it's walking distance from downtown Palo Alto, near the practice's offices, and the hospital—where the group I'm joining works out of.

I continue with my morning texts to Juliette.

Nate: *Gave my two-week notice, not a surprise since my boss knew I was waiting for an offer. Now the hard part, packing up and moving.*

Juliette: *Oops sorry, I can't help you with logistics since I just dropped my phone in my bubble bath. Looks like you shouldn't get a phone wet...*

I bark out a laugh. It's so Juliette. Not overtly sexy, but definitely fun and flirty, giving me a hint of what to expect.

It's nice having someone to text with every morning. More than nice, it makes me feel connected to her. I wouldn't be surprised if other men are pursuing her. I hope I can get to California and close this deal before someone else swoops in and steals her from me.

. . . .

FRIENDS INVITE ME FOR Thanksgiving. Meanwhile, an early season storm is poised to slam into the Midwest on Thanksgiving Day. Making a quick decision, I cancel with friends, find a first-year resident from Salt Lake City, and take off on Wednesday night. We take turns driving, beating out the storm, and making it to his parents in time for Thanksgiving dinner. On Friday, I finish the drive by myself as I land at my sister's.

When I was in town two weeks ago, I didn't contact Jamie. I didn't need a place to stay and I had no interest in explaining my date with

Juliette. I pull into Jamie's tired and exhausted. I trudge up to her, small one-bedroom apartment, looking forward to relaxing. I'm greeted at her door by an unshaven, tatted up, pierced thug wearing a heavy metal T-shirt, shorts and flip-flops—in December, and the whole place reeks of weed.

"Dude, you must be Jamie's big bro."

"Who are you and where's Jamie?"

"Jamie should be back soon; I'm the boyfriend, Tyler, though my friends call me Ty."

Jamie's dating this guy?

What the fuck.

When I stayed here last month he wasn't around.

"All my stuff's on top of—and in-my car. Do you have the opener for her garage?"

"Dude, take it easy. Let's have a beer. Jamie can open it for you when she gets back."

Reluctantly I enter the apartment. ESPN is blaring; there're a couple dead joints in the coffee table ashtray. Tyler hands me a beer as I look him in the eyes.

"Tyler, what do you do for a living?"

Rubbing his hands over his soon-to-be beer belly, he plops himself down on Jamie's couch.

"Workman's comp man, you know, injury."

"Tyler, you look good, what kind of injury do you have?"

"Dude, my back. Man, I fell off a ladder. Messed me up good."

"I take it the pot's to help your back?"

"Yeah, dude, you know marijuana's legal in California."

Where the hell did Jamie find this idiot? I watch about thirty minutes of ESPN, each second Tyler's presence pisses me off more. Jamie comes home, carrying a couple Trader Joe's bags filled with groceries. Our eyes lock, she gives me an uncomfortable smile.

"Nate, you got here earlier than I thought. I see you've met Ty."

Tyler walks up to Jamie, he doesn't take the groceries out of her hands, but puts his arm around her and sticks his tongue in her mouth.

Right in front of me.

I'm about ready to puke or put my fist through his idiotic face. Jamie is smart, athletic, and fun to be around; she's got a great job. What the hell is she thinking?

It's a good thing I moved out here. I'll need to rectify this situation.

I'm not stupid enough to start anything now. Annoyed, I grab the grocery bags from Jamie and place them on the kitchen counter. With her keys in hand, I head downstairs so I can offload my stuff into her garage. When I get back, Tyler is back on the couch watching ESPN as Jamie makes dinner.

Dinner is tense. Jamie gives me the hairy eyeball every time I ask Tyler a question.

After driving for ten hours today, I'm exhausted, though I find it hard to fall asleep. Sleeping on an air mattress in Jamie's living room isn't my problem; it's having to listen to Tyler screw my sister in the next room. I'm using all my will power not to go in her room and kill him. Lucky for him, he's not around when I get up. In dire need of a stress relief, I text Juliette.

Me: *Can I pick you up at noon?*

Juliette: *Yes*

Downstairs, I check my car's oil and then I head to the car wash. The blue paint looks brown from all the dirt and you can barely see out the window. It's the first time I've cleaned my car since this summer. Where a dirty car at this time of year in Minnesota looks normal, here in California, it feels wrong. Everyone else's car shines. The good thing is, thinking about Juliette gets Tyler and my sister out of my mind, putting me in a better mood.

• • • •

WITH A DEEP CALMING breath, I ring Juliette's doorbell. She answers it quickly. Damn, this woman looks good...I want her. My fingers itch to touch her. Today her hair is down, it's shiny, long and flows down her back into big soft curls. With my hands stuffed in my pocket, I control myself from pulling on a coil of hair or running my fingers over that beautiful skin.

"Can you give me an idea of where we're going? I'm not sure what shoes or jacket to bring?" Juliette questions.

I've been so preoccupied with getting here, I never thought about what we're going to do. Mariana would have my ass for being so unprepared. I wing it.

"I haven't been to San Francisco in ages. I thought it might be fun to go up there and be tourists. Do you have to be home at any time?"

"My sister's in town, I spent Thursday and Friday with her and my parents. I think it's cool if I take off for the day, so no plans."

Good, exactly what I was looking forward to, a day with Juliette.

"What do you need to do to get ready?" I ask.

"Give me a minute or two," she responds.

Familiar with that line, I get ready for the long haul of waiting. I head to the couch but am stopped cold in my tracks. The entire dining room wall is covered floor to ceiling in a larger than life-sized painting of her hot roommate. It has to be at least eight feet tall by at ten feet long. Who does something like that?

"Hey," Juliette chirps.

I turn surprised, can she be ready? She was only gone for a minute. I didn't think a woman could get ready so fast.

"Don't you think it's weird she has such a big picture of herself hanging in the dining room?" I ask.

"Don't people in Minnesota have full-size murals of themselves on their dining room walls?" Juliette mugs.

"That has got high maintenance written all over it."

"Yes, that would be an accurate assumption. But, no one goes out with Cassie looking for low maintenance."

"You ready?"

"Do I not look ready?"

"You look great; you took about two minutes to get ready. I only thought guys got ready that fast."

She tips her head and looks at me puzzled. "Let's leave."

On our way up to San Francisco, our conversation is easy. "What do you want to do in San Francisco?" Juliette casually asks as we take the cut off.

My head's not in the game, Mariana would have my balls for not making plans. Casually, I punt, "I'm not quite sure. After sitting in my car for the last two days, I'd like to park and walk around. I thought we could drive to the water."

"Water? That narrows it down. We can park in the Presidio and walk across the Golden Gate Bridge. There's a fancy hotel on the other side in Fort Baker, or we could park at Union Square and walk to Coit Tower, then walk down to the Embarcadero. One direction takes us to Pier 39—you know where all the tourist shops are or we can go in the other direction towards AT&T Park."

"Last time I was in San Francisco I walked across the Golden Gate Bridge. Let's park near Union Square. From there we can start walking. You're cool with walking, right?"

"I wore my favorite boots for walking," she exclaims while lifting up her feet.

We park under Union Square. Once we emerge Juliette looks around as she tries to figure out where we're going, while I pull out my phone and type in *Coit Tower*. Juliette's busy naming streets while my phone lays out the city map. Simultaneously we point in the same direction. This is something else new to get used to. Juliette gets ready fast, knows where she's going and is cool with spontaneous plans. Is this date behavior? When does the crazy control shit kick in?

Feeling happy, I thread my fingers through Juliette's. We walk together to China Town's Dragon Gate. While we wait for the light, I find myself naturally dropping her hand and placing my arm around her shoulders. I pull her just a little bit closer. Her hair smells nice and fruity. It's been way too long since I've been with a woman I wanted.

China Town is a relatively narrow street, filled with people and shops. Most of the shops have bins filled with assorted goods lining their doorway. I've never been much of a shopper or had any interest in collecting things. I pick up a funky silk pouch and hold it up.

"What is this?"

"It's used to store jewelry," Juliette explains.

Interesting, I thought women just left that shit in boxes and all over the counter. A few of the things I pick up and question her about its use, she shrugs.

"How does a merchant sell something when no one knows what it is?" I question.

"I guess we're not their market."

As we get closer to Coit Tower, the road gets steeper and the sidewalk actually turns into stairs.

"How can you drive a car on these steep roads in the winter?" I question.

"This is winter."

"That's right, this will be my first winter without snow."

"We have snow. You just drive to it."

"Do you ski?" I question.

"I love to ski," she responds.

Juliette is getting better and better!

We walk hand in hand across the grounds that lead to Coit Tower. At the line to get in, we fall in behind a hipster couple. The four of us start chatting. The woman picks up one of Juliette's curls. "What do you do to get that color and those types of curls?"

"It comes out of my head that way," Juliette explains, "After swimming this morning, I brushed it and put on some product."

There has to be a hitch. This woman is too casual and easy. The next thing I know we're talking about wine tasting. Juliette doesn't talk about girly things, I wonder if it's because she's an engineer. Mariana and all her friends could talk about hair, nails, and clothes for hours—conversations that make me want to scream, or do what I did, leave and go work out.

At the top of the tower, there's a panoramic view of San Francisco Bay and the Embarcadero. Juliette leans on the railing as we both look down at the waterfront. Unable to resist myself, I pick up one of her curls and twist it around my finger. It feels silky and smooth. She tilts her head and looks at me sweetly. I take in her smooth luminescent skin as I drag the pads of my finger down her cheek to her jaw. The warmth of her skin ignites my entire body.

Which makes me wonder, what does she taste like? Is the rest of her body as soft and sweet as her face? Slowly she licks her sweet pink lips. Silently I gasp. My mind momentarily short circuits. I try to recover by thinking of things that will keep my libido in control...work...my apartment...purchasing furniture...a new bed...Juliette in my bed. This isn't working. We need to move.

"Come on; let's check out the other views," I suggest as I grasp her hand and move us around the structure. After we've made a complete loop, I look out towards the water, which gives me an idea. "Let's head to the Embarcadero and get a drink. I'd like to sit out on the pier."

Pulling out my phone, I read through the restaurant choices.

"Do you like oysters?"

"Yeah, I'll eat almost anything."

How come that doesn't surprise me? Firmly grasping Juliette's hand in mine, we walk down the tower, through the park, finally landing on the wide sidewalk that lines the busy Embarcadero. This area reminds me of Chicago. For four years I lived right on Lake Michigan. I loved being part of all the people down by the waterfront.

It's about a twenty-minute walk to the restaurant. They seat us on their outdoor patio overlooking the water. As I pick up the menu, Juliette rubs her hands together.

"What's hot?" she asks.

"You're cold?"

"Yeah, I have a little engine that easily runs cold. You have a lot more muscle mass than me."

She is a little thing. I pull off my jacket and wrap it around her. She looks sexy, dwarfed by the size of my jacket.

"Wasn't Irish coffee invented in San Francisco?" I question.

"Yeah, over at the Buena Vista by Ghirardelli Square."

"I bet they can make it well here."

I watch as Juliette snuggles into my coat, lucky coat. Doing the next best thing I pick up her hands, they feel petite and cold as I rub them between mine. Juliette peers up at me through her eyelashes and then bites her lip. I inwardly sigh from anticipation.

"Better?" I ask with a voice that sounds low to my ears. With a shy smile, she nods.

"What can I get you folks?" our server interrupts.

· · · ·

WHEN WE FINALLY DECIDE to leave the restaurant, Juliette hands me back my jacket. I reluctantly take it, then use the opportunity to tug her near so I can keep her warm. Well, actually, I tuck her close because I like the way she feels.

Back on the Embarcadero, I point to the Ferry Building.

"Let's take a ferry to Sausalito," I suggest. Juliette agreeably nods.

The horn blows for the next boat as I purchase our tickets. Quickly I grab ahold of Juliette's hand.

"Let's run for it," I exclaim.

Once on the ferry, we find a bench that overlooks a large portal, which is more like a picture window. Strategically I place my arm around her as I tuck her close, drawing lazy circles on her arm while I fantasize about making love to her. One by one the other people in this cabin leave.

"Juliette," I whisper,

She peers up at me through her long, dark, lashes. Her lips, that have been tantalizing all day, feel like magnates to my steel. I move close enough to kiss her. With an overwhelming need to feel her warmth, I grab her knee and wrap her leg over mine.

Her mouth tastes like oysters and coffee as our tongues meet. The sensation is pure sex. I have an overwhelming desire to consume her. I brush my tongue against hers and enjoy as the glow of sex runs through me. It feels like I could continue kissing her like this forever, as her taste and the proximity of her body ignites me. My reverie is interrupted by the loud padding of little feet and screams of children. Reluctantly, I release those lips as a couple of kids plaster themselves against the window in front of us. Before their parents show up I unwrap us.

The dad joins his kids and immediately his eyes zero in on mine. He narrows his eyes, as he shoots me a *behave yourself in front of my kids* look. Juliette leans into me, I can feel her pulse race. Her fingers gently massage my leg, which is driving me crazy. It's not like I want her to stop, it's just I don't want to stand up.

When the ferry finally docs I wait until our area empties. Reluctantly I stand up and extending my hand to Juliette. I thread my fingers through hers as we walk silently to the exit. As we wait to debark, I wrap my arms around her shoulders, pulling her close, which gives me the perfect opportunity to smell her hair again and feel her form against mine. Man, having her so close is killing me.

The two of us walk together through the fancy little Sausalito shops. Our conversation is light and easy. As the sun lowers, I start thinking about what's next. It will be dinner time when we get back to

San Francisco. As Juliette casually looks at some artwork, I pull out my phone and search for a restaurant, make the reservations, and then set an alarm so that we don't miss the last ferry back. After performing all my planning activities, I look around, quickly spotting Juliette with a contemplative look on her face.

She's standing in front of a large Doctor Seuss; *Sam I Am* illustration. Unable to keep my hands off her, I wrap them around her shoulders and pull her against my chest.

"Do you remember when that Senator filibustered against ACA?" I nod as she continues. "During the filibuster, he read his kids *Green Eggs and Ham*. I never got that. He went to Princeton and Harvard; how could he have failed to get that the point of the book was to open up and give something new a chance."

"I thought the point of the book was the power of perseverance in the face of stubborn resistance."

"Even so, that wouldn't have supported his argument, since it's all based on the point of view who's being stubborn and who's persevering? Wouldn't he have done better if he had read *Horton Hears a Who*? That's about those in power listening to the powerless."

"Didn't that happen a while ago?"

"Yeah, I was taking a civics class, that's why I remember. What drives me crazy is when someone uses the wrong analogy. Now, every time I look at *Green Eggs and Ham* I think of that guy."

"Like Irony instead of, what did you say—oxymoron?"

"Was I wrong or did I extend a concept? Doesn't oxymoron mean the opposite, while ironic is the opposite of what you expect? So, oxymoron would be a sign on that steep mountain saying easy grade, while ironic would be a guy who rides his bike to the top and smokes a cigarette. Does the English language even have a word that means conflicting activities?"

"I think we have two words, conflicting activities."

"In grad school, I had a friend from Germany. Her English vocabulary was amazing. She always complained that her vocabulary was limited. At sunrise we were running at the Dish, she looked at the Santa Cruz mountains, pointed and said, 'In German, we have a word, '*Blauschimmer*'. It means the way the hills turn from pink to blue at sunrise. I don't know what the English equivalent is.'"

"I get your point, I don't think we have one specific word for conflicting activities."

Of course, I immediately compare Juliette to Mariana, which isn't easy, they're very different, which thankfully is probably a sign I've moved on. Maybe our breakup was for the best. Maybe Jamie was right. Being with Juliette is so easy and I think we share more in common.

My phone's alarm pulls me to the present, reminding me to catch our ferry. Juliette and I find the same seat, in front of the big window. We watch the lights of San Francisco grow close. This isn't a vacation, I remind myself, I'm living here, this is my new life.

After dinner, Juliette offers to pay her share. I'm glad she doesn't take me for granted. But, I don't want there to be any ambiguity.

"It's not a date if you pay, and this is definitely a date," I declare.

"What do you mean?"

"I might be new in the area, but I'm not looking for another friend."

When we get back to my Jeep, I have all good intentions of being the perfect gentleman. Gallantly I open the passenger door. But Damn...I've been good all day...And she smells so nice...And looks so pretty.

My lizard brain takes over. The next thing I know I've backed her into the car, block her in and placed my hands on either side of her head. My eyes graze over her pretty face, while my focus narrows on those luscious pink lips. Slowly her pink tongue darts out and slides over her top lip. I crash my lips into hers, my tongue following the path I just watched hers take. With a deep breath, I take in her scent. Her mouth opens and I dart my tongue along hers. It feels soft and warm, it tastes good, female. I bet she's tight. My hand darts down to her waist as I pull her close, kiss her harder, deeper, that overwhelming desire to consume her returns. She runs her hands over my arm and chest. I like the feel of her fingers on me as she grabs my shirt and tugs me closer.

Kissing doesn't relieve my need, it only makes me hungry for more, as I contemplate how to get what I crave.

"Get a room," some juvenile shouts from a passing car.

His voice jolts us back to reality, breaking the spell.

Slowly I release our kiss and place my forehead against hers. I breathe in her warm, sweet smell.

"Juliette," I moan.

"Nate," she purrs.

Her voice sends shivers down my back. I want her so bad. Slowly I rub my cheek against her soft skin.

"We should get in the car, we should go back," I whisper into her hair.

This woman has possessed me.

How can it be?

I barely know her.

I kiss her ear, her jaw, then rub my nose along her cheek. Gently she responds by kissing my lips.

"Yes," she whispers into my mouth.

"Yeah, we should either get a room or get in the car," I groan.

"Car. We should get in the car," she moans back.

Back in the day, I would have never chosen to go after a girl like Juliette. That's because she would have never been open for a hookup. Then again, that's why I want her so bad. I gather my willpower, finally pulling away from what I crave.

With a deep inner sigh, I open the passenger door.

The sexual energy in the car is palpable. We listen to the music. I don't think either of us can speak.

I pull up to her place, she releases her buckle.

"Today was great, really great," she gushes.

Winding one of her curls around my finger until my hand reaches her face, I run my knuckles along her jaw, "Yeah, it was a great day."

My gaze wanders to her mouth. She gasps. Our mouths meet, I relish her warmth and taste. When I release the kiss, I already know I want more. My lips land on her soft face, ending by her ear.

"Juliette," I moan.

She shivers.

I move her hair, exposing her neck, layering a line of kisses down to her shoulder. My body vibrates from craving. I want her. But a small inner voice yells from deep inside my brain, be cool, don't overplay your hand, there's time. My libido fights with my mind. Libido wins, my lips move back to hers.

She softly moans.

Man, I want her even more. My fingers search out the soft curves and the heat of her body as our mouths devour each other.

"Juliette, I want you," I whisper.

She pushes against my chest. "I need to go inside."

"Can I join you?" I plead.

She stares at me through her eyelashes, slowly shaking her head. "Not this time; not this night."

"Tomorrow, can I see you tomorrow?" I plead again.

"I'd like that," she purrs.

"I'll text you in the morning."

"I look forward to it," she replies, then demurely bites her lip.

Man, I want to bite that lip too.

But I watch, unable to stop her as she grabs her purse, fishes out her keys, opens the car door. My eyes catch movement... a figure standing across the street. It's a man; he's obviously been watching us. Not something I like.

With my eyes firmly on the guy, awareness quickly takes over.

"Who's that?"

Juliette stills, she lets out a small gasp. It's apparent when the guy realizes we've noticed him, he uncomfortably moves. Now I can see his face.

"I don't know," Juliette whispers in a soft voice.

All my MME instincts move to the forefront. Maintaining eye contact I quickly I get out of my Jeep and assume a warrior attitude. With a stern voice and with killer eye contact, I bring my voice two octaves lower.

"Can I help you?"

The guy's body position screams discomfort. "I'm waiting for Cassie."

Juliette leans towards me, "Oh that must be the guy Cassie had a fling with."

"Cassie's not home, you better move on." I coolly instruct. Leaning towards Juliette my voice is firm, "Let me walk you to your door." Keeping a wary eye out, I walk Juliette to her door and watch her enter. "Lock up," I instruct. "Call the police if you see him around again."

After I hear the door lock, I stand guard for a few minutes. Once in my Jeep, I circle the block to make sure he's actually taken off.

$$\bullet\ \bullet\ \bullet\ \bullet$$

ON A GOOD NOTE, I GET back to Jamie's late enough that I don't have to hear my sister and Tyler doing it in her bedroom. My apartment is available on Monday. First thing Monday morning I'm ordering a bed. The less time I stay at my sister's the better; though I'm still going to set her straight on this guy. What on earth could she possibly be thinking?

In the morning, my soon-to-be new boss sends me a text, *I have two Shark tickets for tonight's game. My wife and I were going to go. Call me by noon if you can use them.*

Cool, I love hockey, and even better, I now have a plan for my date. I love when life works out.

Jamie and I spend a couple of hours online choosing furniture. Tomorrow I'll get everything else that I need. While Jamie and I are in front of the computer, Tyler is sitting on the sofa getting high as he watches ESPN, what a looser. I'll take Jamie out for dinner this week to talk about Tyler.

In the afternoon Juliette answers the door all friendly, but shy. She blushes and turns her head when I enter. She must be thinking something naughty, which is nice. I drag my fingers down her pretty face and enjoy watching her shudder in response. Since touching her only makes me want her more, I pull her close for a nice long kiss. Using sizeable self-control, I finally pull away.

"Let's eat," I murmur, when what I really want, is to pick her up, find her bed, and screw her until neither of us can move.

Dinner goes well. Each time we're together it gets easier, more relaxed.

"Are you a hockey fan?" I ask as we head to the Shark Tank.

"No, this is the first game I've ever been to."

"But you've watched hockey on TV?"

"No, but I looked it up on Wikipedia, it doesn't look that much different the soccer, right?"

"Yeah, similar."

This should be an interesting night. I pray she doesn't talk about lame shit the entire time. Maybe taking her was a mistake. My sister follows the sport, but...I really want to spend more time with Juliette.

Our tickets are amazing, three rows behind the bench. Juliette and my seats are at the end of the row. I situate Juliette so she sits on the far side of the partners and physical therapists.

As the game starts, I lean into Juliette. "This morning I checked out a couple of places to work out. There's one walking distance from my future apartment that looks cool. There are also some great restaurants in the area."

"Aren't you going to watch the game?" Juliette questions as she points to the ice.

Damn, I like this woman.

"Off sides," Juliette asks about five minutes later. "In soccer, you're offsides when an attacking player goes behind the line of defenders before the ball has been kicked to them. I was reading about hockey and I'm totally confused by the rules?"

I explain the blue line to her, then spend the rest of the game breaking down player strategy, showing her how the guys are either doing it well or messing up.

On my other side are a couple of doctors. They point out the players and inform me each of the surgeries they've performed. One of the team's trainers comes over to talk to us. Luckily, no one gets injured during the game. They played a good game; better yet, I look forward to taking Juliette again. I illegally park in front of her place. This time I don't even ask if I can come inside. My only goal for tonight is to keep her in the car kissing me for as long as I can.

• • • •

FIRST THING MONDAY morning I get my apartment key, unload my personal possessions and shop for what I need. Once settled, I text Jamie: *Dinner tomorrow, your choice, I treat.*

Jamie and I meet at a Cuban restaurant in Mid Town Palo Alto. We each get a beer as we toast to living near each other. My sister is great; I have no idea why she's going out with Tyler. Not thinking too deeply about this before dinner, I wait until we both have had a drink and have eaten some dinner, before I broach the subject.

"How long have you been seeing Tyler?"

"Why do you ask?"

"You never mentioned a boyfriend. Last month when I was here, he wasn't around. When I show up, I see you're living with this guy. You're my sister; I want to know more about him."

"Nate, don't give me your shit. I like Ty."

"What? I'm just asking. Do you have anything in common with this guy?"

"This is like the pot calling the kettle black."

"What does that mean?"

"Really, I know you. You've been giving Ty that look of yours. The 'I'm going to beat the shit out of you' look you get. This is my life; Ty makes me happy, just leave it."

"You're better than this guy. I don't want to see you get involved with some—"

"Really, you're in no position to judge, not after you get yourself *engaged* to Mariana."

"What the hell does that mean? Mariana had a job."

"Your issue with Ty is his job?"

"That's a start."

"Your other issue is his tattoos? You have tattoos."

"Not the tattoos."

"Look, Mariana was a whack job and you wanted to marry her. You have no room to say anything about Ty to me."

I settle back in my chair as I realize that I'm handling this situation all wrong. Any issue I have with Ty, Jamie brings up Mariana. Why didn't Jamie ever like her? How do I get Jamie to dump this guy?

"I get it," Jamie says. "Ty rubs you the wrong way. I never gave you shit for Mariana, even though I never liked how she treated you, and the two of you had nothing in common."

"We had lots in common."

"What, name three things you liked to do with each other...out of the sack?"

"This conversation is about you and Tyler, not about me and Mariana."

"Can't you come up with even one thing? Ty treats me well, he's easy to be with, we have fun times, he might not have much ambition, but it's nice being with someone who thinks I'm great."

"You are great." This elicits an eye roll.

"Mariana treated me well."

"Mariana spent her day ordering you around 'lmao get this for me, lmao buy this for me, lmao do this for me, and lmao take care of me.' What did that chick ever do for you?"

"She made me happy."

"Ty makes me happy. Leave it alone Nate. It's not like I'm planning on having his babies."

"Then I hope you're using an IUD. You know they have a much lower failure rate than the pill."

"I'm not discussing contraception with my brother, ever!"

On Friday morning, I start my day by texting Juliette. I was bummed she was busy every night this week. Then again, my overloaded schedule was a sticking point with Mariana. Maybe if I date a woman who is busy, things will work out better. For our Friday date, I book reservations at a restaurant one of the nurses recommends. I walk from where I park to Juliette's, I can't help but notice how warm the air is. It's hard for me to believe that this really is December.

Juliette answers her door wearing a tight scoop neck sweater, which kind of takes my breath away. "Hi," is about all I can say before I lose self-control and pull her close. Gently cupping her head, I brush my knuckle down her beautiful cheek. With a long, deep kiss I hear myself moan from pleasure. When we break the kiss, I groan.

"I'd really like to continue this in your room but I made reservations. We should head to the restaurant."

She responds with a sexy shudder. "Today was cold; I should grab a warm jacket."

"It's December, I can't believe Californians are complaining about how cold it is. Do you realize there are still leaves on the trees and the temperature's been in the fifties?"

"Yeah, that's what I mean, today never got warmer than the mid-fifties. They're talking about the lows tonight getting down to the thirties. That's really cold when you're on the pool deck wearing only flip-flops and a swimsuit."

"Wait, what? You swim outdoors at dawn? Now?"

"The pool's eighty, it's the deck that's freezing. Anyways we don't have indoor pools."

"When it comes to weather you are the toughest and wimpiest person I've ever met," I exclaim.

"You've got a lot to learn about living in California. It's a lot different than visiting California," she responds.

"That sounds like a lesson I'll enjoy learning." I pull her in tight for another kiss before we take off to walk the few blocks to the restaurant.

The restaurant serves Spanish and South American food. I order a Malbec. Isn't this what Mariana and I drank on our first date? Stop obsessing on Mariana, that's over.

Juliette and I take turns choosing an assortment of small plate tapas to share. After eating, I catch Juliette looking pensive. I reach across the table for her hand. The sensation of her skin on mine sends a thrill to my core. Gently I rub my thumb against her soft warm skin.

"Hey, I think I lost you, what are thinking about?"

"You're not like Bon Jovi from *Sex in the City*, right?" she blurts out.

"Come again? What does some rock star from the eighties, and a TV show from the nineties have to do with me?"

"Saying it out loud does make it sound kind of crazy. Bon Jovi's character sleeps with Carrie. Afterward, he tells her he loses interest in a woman after he's had sex. You're not one of those guys; that's into the chase then gets bored once he captures the prey?"

Okay, she totally lost me with the Bon Jovi reference but she wants to know if I'm a player. Before Mariana, I was a player. I would never have wasted my time on dinner or chosen this woman. But I've grown up, I want a relationship, I want her.

"I was wondering when we were going to have this conversation. I like that you didn't want to sleep with me right away." Shaking my head, I can't help but chuckle, since last weekend all I wanted, was to screw her. "I would have liked it if you wanted to sleep with me right away, but it's nice to take it slow for a change. You don't come across as a sexual adventuress." I might be exposing myself, but if I want to be in an adult relationship, I need to be clear and honest. "No, I'm not interested in sleeping with you once, then moving on. It's way too early to make any promises, but I would like to get to know you more."

The air between us is thick. I lean in and twirl one of her curls between my fingers, the softness feels good, I have an overriding desire to feel her skin as I profess the opposite of what I really want, "But I won't rush you. We can take this as slow or as fast as you want."

"There's no current girlfriend or wife back in Minnesota?"

"No current girlfriend or wife back in Minnesota." Gently I brush my thumb over her long thin fingers. "Any boyfriends or husband I should know about?"

"I'm single. No current attachments. I don't share. If you want to sleep with me, you can't be sleeping with anyone else."

"Yeah, I can live with that. I don't share either."

Our waiter shows up, interrupting our intimacy as he asks about dessert. Juliette shakes her head. I do too. My only thought is how quickly can I get Juliette back to her place and get her in bed.

"Why don't we go back to my place?" Juliette coos.

I almost throw my credit card at the waiter. As quick as I can, I sign the bill, grab my jacket and hold my hand out for Juliette.

"You coming?" I say.

Tucking her in close, we walk the few blocks back to her place, I remind myself to breathe and take this slowly, as I try to control my heightened anticipation. My eyes are targeted on her. She unlocks and opens the front door. Lizard brain takes over as we both step inside. Instantly I block her against the wall, kicking the door closed. With one hand on the wall I balancing myself and pull her close. We kiss hard and deep. She moans into my mouth.

"I want you," I growl.

She pulls me tight as we kiss, and she pulls off my coat. Gently I rub my cheek against her soft cheek as I work on her jacket. My hands itch to touch her smooth skin. I search for the hem of her sweater. Her cold fingers run up my back. Surprisingly I like it, since it causes me to shudder.

"I don't want your roommate walking in on us, can we move to your bedroom?" I manage to murmur.

Kissing her ear, then sucking on her ear lobe, I could eat this sweet woman up as my lips move down to her neck. She smells wonderful and tastes even better. She pulls away and grabs my hand, flashing me a sly look as she leads me to her bedroom.

Her room has ambient light from the street, not as bright as I want but I'm not about to stop touching her to turn the lights on. Wanting more skin, I run my hands along the rim of her sweater, grasping it firmly I pull it off her, then run my fingers up her back and release her bra. I've always been a breast guy and Juliette's are wonderful; large, round and perky. My mouth and fingers ache to fondle them.

Meanwhile, Juliette is working to get my shirt off, not an easy feat since I'm caressing her amazing breasts. We break our kiss. I take the break to get my shirt off and look at her tits. Her unlatched bra is covering them; dragging my fingertips from her neck down her arm, unveils what I crave. I give myself a moment to take them in. The live woman in front of me is so much better than the image from TV and all my fantasies. The urge to feel her skin overtakes my desire to look at her. With my index finger, I grab the waistband of her jeans and pull her close. With one hand I undo her jeans, while I use the other to continue exploring her breasts.

Juliette undoes my pants, touching me through my boxers, almost making me come. Kissing the spot where her neck meets her shoulder, she rolls her head, moans, then gives me access, as I lick her from shoulder to ear. Something about the salty sweet taste of female skin heightens my craving. Her whole body starts shuddering. Now I'm conflicted, do I want to look at her or touch her? Not wanting to think about this too hard, I pull down her jeans, back her up on the bed, and gently lay her down. I run my hand down her leg until I reach her boot. I tug on her heel.

"Zipper, you need to pull down the zipper," she moans out.

Happily I comply. I pull off her boots, jeans, and socks. Her body lies before me, almost naked. She's beautiful; her skin glows in the soft gray light, calling me to touch her. Dragging my fingertips slowly up her legs, I run my fingers against her folds, I can feel she's soaked right through her panties. Good, she wants it as bad as I do. Recklessly I pull off her panties and then quickly shed the rest of my clothes.

"I hope you want me to continue," I plead, not wanting to stop. Her large eyes take me in as she solemnly nods.

"Yes," she whispers.

I silently cheer. "You will tell me if you want me to stop."

My gaze moves up the length of her beautiful body. I lean in, kiss and lick her core. Her body shudders from my touch; her skin feels warm, sweet and salty, the human equivalent of fresh kettle corn. I relish the view, looking up at her face through her large breasts. I inch on up so one of my hands can freely explore her breast as I balance myself with the other. My hand on her breast is the happiest, luckiest hand ever. Licking her other breast, I draw her nipple into my mouth and suck hard. My eyes flash up to watch her expression. Her head goes back exposing the white column of her neck as a deep moan fills the air.

Her sounds go directly to my dick, as I tell it to wait its turn, I'm enjoying this too much to end it too quickly. My hands and mouth are both playing with her rack, she arches her back; the thrill of her reaction runs a line of anticipation down my core.

"You have amazing breasts, I could get lost in these breasts," I mumble in appreciation.

Even though all I crave is to be inside of her. I want her to say it, I want her to want me.

"You still want me to continue?"

"Yes," she gasps out.

Pleasure mixed with pure lust screams through my body, as my dick aches for release.

"Good," I respond, it would kill me to stop now.

"Can we continue under the comforter where it's warmer?" she manages to emit between moans.

I nod, as I watch her hot ass race under the covers. Joining her, I run my hands down her curves, as I enjoy the feeling of her thighs, hips, up to her waist. I relish the female body, nothing feels so good. She places a leg over my leg opening herself up to me as she runs her hand down to my hard-on. I gasp. I run my fingers through her landing strip of pubic hair. Mariana used to shave everything when she wore her skimpy bikinis. It always freaked me out, like she was a child, not an adult. I'm only interested in being with a woman, a soft, round woman.

Juliette runs a finger along my dick, twirling it around the end. Not a good idea since I'm at the edge. I know what I crave, what I want, the feeling of her wrapped around my dick shivering and quaking below me. But I can wait. I want this to be good.

My fingers find her nub and unhood it, when it's exposed, I gently pet it. Immediately she responds, bucking against my hand and moaning. My blood rushes with satisfaction, while her body quivers and builds.

"Come for me," I softly implore, "I want to feel you come on my hand."

I can feel her stomach contract. My dick is so jealous of my fingers, but I maintain the friction by exploring her tight, warm, wet core.

I suck on her nipple, pulling it long in my teeth. Her panting is intense as she adds in these groaning noises. Happiness fills me as I enjoy my new playground. Releasing her breast from my mouth, I blow gently over the wet skin as I watch her eyes squint and her mouth open into an O, as the orgasm rolls through her. I'm a lucky guy to get to touch and watch this pretty woman.

"Are you up for more? I softly ask as she starts to come down, "Can I join you this time?"

She nods, my inner voice screams *good girl*. Our mouths join. Our tongues dance as my dick screams to join in. Releasing her briefly I reach over the bed, down to my pants, pulling a condom out of my wallet. I return to her side, she gives me a sweet smirk.

"Optimistic," she purrs.

"Forever hopeful."

My balls must be blue, with a hiss I roll on the condom. Even so, I want to hear her beg for it.

"Are you sure you want this?"

"Yeah, I want this with you."

"Good, I'll take it easy."

Rolling her on her back, I lean in for a deep satisfying kiss as I gently stroke her folds with my dick. Each stroke going a little deeper, a little harder. She feels wet, warm, soft, and incredibly tight. Carefully, at first, I rock into her. Cheek to cheek the air is alive with our hard breathing. Her mouth is by my ear as she squeaks in pleasure. I increase the rhythm as her muscles squeeze my dick. Wanting to rock deeper, I bring her knees up to her chest and feel her spasm. My lower back tightens, the spasm moves down to my balls. Man, there isn't anything that feels as good as orgasming together. As I pump into her she spasms on the entire length of my dick. As she milks my dick, my brain goes blank, the tension peaks, as I release.

As my dick relaxes, I pull out while she continues to shake and gasp. It always amazes me how different men and women orgasm. It takes a while to get a woman going, but you know you've done it right if it takes a while for her to come down. I find post-coital bliss in holding a woman when she's on the way down.

Rolling onto my back, I thread my fingers through hers. A slow, happy smile spreads across my face as my body and mind relax, complete satisfaction. Still wanting to feel that soft sweet body against me, I pull Juliette close and kiss her forehead.

"That was good, really good."

Damn, that was an understatement that was amazing. When her body relaxes and my mind starts returning to normal it hits me, I never locked the front door.

With a grunt I get up, head to the living room, lock the door, and pick up our jackets. Back in her bedroom, I drop our jackets in the corner and climb back in bed, I want that sweet body wrapped around me as I fall asleep.

* * * *

THE FAMILIAR DING OF my phone's alarm blasts me awake. It takes me a moment to realize where I am. I'm in Juliette's bed. I search around, find my pants and grab the phone out of the pocket. Juliette rolls over, as I turn my gaze to her, she gives me a sweet smile.

"Sorry, I didn't mean to wake you."

She drags her finger down my chest, which turns my dick back on.

"I think it would have freaked me out more if I woke up and you were gone."

I like the way she looks just waking up with her just fucked hair and mascara flaked around her eyes.

"Last night was good. I'm not leaving quickly."

Lightly I peck on her cheek, then lick her ear as she bends her shoulder and giggles. Man, I want her so bad. What the hell was I thinking when I told them I'd show up for this surgery, I don't even officially start work until Monday.

"Juliette, can I interest you in a quick one before I take off for work?" I plead.

She snickers as her finger runs around the design of my tat, a definite turn on.

"Yeah, a quick one would be fun."

Damn, this woman is amazing. I reach back down to the floor as I grab another condom out of my back pocket. We softly kiss as I roll it over my twitching dick.

She flinches from excitement as I work her clit. When she's coming, I work her a little harder before I thrust inside of her. Her shuddering body feels great. We start off slowly, she feels tight on my dick as I stroke into her. As my pace increases, we get in this amazing rhythm. I wait until she's in full orgasm before I let myself release and ride the waves of bliss.

When my breathing returns to normal, I pull her tight.

"That was a nice way to wake up," I whisper into her ear as I watch her shudder.

Damn, I want to spend the day in bed with this woman. What was I thinking? If they weren't expecting me, I'd blow this surgery off. Sometimes I hate reality.

"Unfortunately I've got to run," I reluctantly explain.

After I dress, I can't resist moving the covers to get one more look at her rocking body. Then I pull myself away to tug on my socks and shoes. My fingers gravitate back to her warm soft skin as I run my fingers around her tit.

"I'll be done at two, I'll text. You're free this afternoon, right?"

She slowly nods as she lets out a small moan.

• • • •

AT THE CLINIC, A NURSE escorts me to where I can scrub in. There are a number of surgeries scheduled for today. We break quickly for lunch and discuss the afternoon schedule. When I get out of the OR at three, it hits me, I forgot to text Juliette at lunch. I'm falling off my game; Mariana would have had my head for a mistake like that.

Me: *Got stuck in surgery, heading home now."*

She's been cool, even so, I hope I don't screw things up before we get started.

Juliette: *I'm at the arena in Los Altos Hills working with horses. Meet me here when you're ready.*

I make a point to reload on the condoms; I'm looking forward to tonight, and no plans tomorrow.

• • • •

THE AIR IS COOL, THE light is moving towards dusk when I finally arrive. Instantly I spot Juliette. She's in the arena with six horses, an older woman, and a couple of girls. She waves to me, we meet at the fence.

"Good timing, we were just about to head back to the stables," she says.

Mariana would be cutting me a new one if I showed up two hours late. I'm not sure why I'm getting off so easy, but I'm not about to question her. Being this close to her makes my nervous system light up, while my dick twitches in recognition. The closer she gets, the more control I have to exert, since I want her so bad. I casually lean against the fence, reach my hand out and brush her cheek with the tips of my fingers. With my index finger on the underside of her chin, I pull her close until our lips meet. In the background, I can hear the teenage girls giggling.

Juliette's pupils dilate and she bites her bottom lip. It takes her a couple seconds to recover.

"We have a choice," Juliette explains. "I can leave Deborah with two teenagers and six horses, or you can help us bring the horses back to the stables. Deborah will bring us back here to get our cars."

"I've never ridden before."

"Then we'll give you an easy horse."

"Okay, sure I'll try it."

"Nate will help us take them back," Juliette yells to the woman who looks to be around my mom's age. She turns back to me. "It's going to get cold, let me see if Deborah has extra gloves and ear muffs."

"I've got some in my car."

"You are a boy scout, all prepared for cold weather."

Boy scout, where I've been living you better have back-up gear or you could freeze to death. After retrieving my spare hat and gloves I jog to the center of the arena. Juliette hands me a helmet.

"Which one do I ride?"

Juliette takes me by my hand and leads me to a big brown horse. "This is Jackson; he's a very sweet horse. We need to keep Velvet busy so she doesn't see the others leave."

Juliette unhitches a big spotted horse that I assume is Velvet and turns both horses so they're facing away from the group that's leaving. After the other riders have left, Juliette shows me how to get on Jackson, how to turn left, turn right, stop, and how to perform an emergency dismount. Juliette leads the two horses, one with me on his back, to the gate.

"It's almost four thirty, we have about twenty minutes before the sun completely sets, she explains. "Hopefully we'll get to the barn before it's pitch dark."

She strings battery-operated lights over the horses' necks and hands me a safety vest with a battery powered light bar. Her horse is even bigger than mine and is acting restless. I'm wondering if this little woman can handle such a big horse. She mounts easily. Immediately her horse calms down; how'd she do that?

"You need to be on my left side," she explains.

Juliette moves my horse's rope to her right hand. Somehow, she gets the horses walking down the road though I don't see how she does it.

"How long will this take?" I question.

"About forty minutes," she answers.

We walk the horses a couple of blocks on the street, then enter a rural path. I look for trail markings or signs. Nothing, should I get out my phone? I'd hate for us to get lost.

"Are you sure you know the way back?" I ask.

"These horses take this path almost every day. They know dinners at the other end of the trail. I guarantee they know the way home."

We ride silently as the light from the setting sun turns the mountains pink, the sky purple, and the ground a soft gray. It's a spectacular show. The sun sets further and the trail becomes dark. The lights around the horses' necks cast an eerie glow. This is amazing. Am I really riding a horse through the hills at sunset? The setting sun reminds me of the conversation we had in Sausalito.

"Blauschimmer, wasn't that the word your German friend had for the pink hills at dawn and dusk?"

"Yeah, I'm glad I get to share one of my favorite times of day and places with you."

The path smells wonderful— earth and plants. The air is brisk and still. The clomping sound the horse hoofs makes the evening feel timeless. We start losing the pink cast as the trees become backlit against the sky. It's like entering an old western movie. The air gets colder while the only illumination is the blue and green lights strung around the horses' necks and the light from our vests. Periodically we pass lights of a house in the distance. My horse neighs and the next thing I know Deborah has taken Jackson's lead rope. When I dismount I hear the teenage girls giggle as they run to a waiting car.

"You're a hit with teens," Juliette teases.

We walk the horses to the barn where she shows me how to tie the horses' rope to a hitch. Juliette and Deborah quickly and expertly take everything off the horses. Deborah shows me how to flip the saddle pads and place each of the saddles on a large peg. Juliette hands me some round brushes with straps for handles.

"This is my favorite part. I love grooming the horses. I think it's because the horses enjoy being groomed." She proceeds to show me how to wipe down their coats.

Helping Deborah put on the horses' blankets, I watch Juliette checks their hooves. These horses are huge, Juliette moves around them with no fear. Finally, she leads them to their stalls. Before this evening, I never considered riding a horse, but after tonight, I can see how people become hooked. Tonight's already been wonderful, and I've yet to touch her.

After Deborah drops us off by the arena, I walk Juliette to her car.

"Do you want to meet me at my place?" she offers.

I answer with a deep kiss.

• • • •

SUDDENLY I'M AWAKE, from the light I can tell it's the middle of the night. It takes me a second to realize where I am. I'm in Juliette's bed. A memory from last night flashes through my mind. It's skin, and lips, gasping and pumping. Instantly my dick twitches. I reach my hand out and feel the warmth coming off of Juliette as she soundly sleeps. I'm jolted by the noise of a door closing followed by high-pitched laughter.

It's clearly the sound of a man and women in the living room. It must be Juliette's roommate. After a few minutes, they head to the master bedroom. I start falling back to sleep. The undeniable sounds of hard core sex, play right through the wall. How can Juliette sleep through this?

The sex gets wilder and the roommate starts screaming, which finally wakes Juliette up.

"That's your roommate, right?" I whisper.

"Oh, that's her all right," she giggles.

"They came in about a half an hour ago."

"How long have they been at it?"

"I'm not sure what they were doing before, but the screaming just started."

Now I'm wide-awake with a beautiful, naked, woman inches from me. I don't hesitate, I pull her on top of me. We start kissing. But are jolted apart from a series of screams coming through the wall, from the very loud sex going on next door.

"Is she usually like this?"

"She's usually at his place. But yeah, I've learned to keep my earbuds ready. I really don't need this much information."

The roommate is now yelling out explicit directions. I run my hands over all the nice soft curves draped over my naked body.

"She sure knows what she wants."

"It's much funnier listening to her when you're lying naked in bed next to a hot guy."

My dick, which was warming up, jumps to attention.

"Is all their loud noise turning you on?" Juliette asks.

"No, lying naked in bed with all this soft, warm skin is turning me on."

We listen to a few more screams. "It's been going on for a while. What do you think he's doing to her?" she whispers.

"I'm not sure, but I can make some rather wild guesses."

"Like what?"

Memories of some of the wilder women I've slept with flash through my mind.

"Maybe he's touching her here." I grab her tit with my mouth and suck hard, stretching out her tit with my teeth, which elicits a deep gasp. "That didn't cause a scream. Either I'm doing it wrong or you're not a screamer."

"You are definitely not doing anything wrong," she gasps.

"That's good to know." I lean in and lick her clavicle. "Mmm, you sure taste good." I kiss up her neck, making sure to hit all the sensitive spots as my fingers explore her folds. As she comes undone, I throw her knees over my shoulders and we make a little noise of my own.

• • • •

THE SUN STREAMING IN the window wakes me up. I'm alone in bed. I grab my bag and head into the bathroom where I interrupt a naked Juliette brushing her teeth. Now that's a good visual. I like all that cream-colored skin. My finger runs along her tan lines as I lean in and kiss her shoulder. Since that felt so good, I rub her nice round hips and ass.

"Can I interest you in a shower?" I murmur.

"Yeah, some nice clean fun," she eagerly responds.

Once I brush my teeth, I now want to taste her. I pull her in tight for a deep kiss. She places her hands on either side of my mouth.

"A little too prickly for you?" I chuckle.

Juliette watches me shave, which almost causes me to cut myself since it's hard to maintain focus, with all those naked female curves so close. As soon as I'm done shaving, I pull her tight. Every fiber in me wants to feel all that smooth, soft skin against my body again.

"How about you get that shower going, and I'll join you in a second."

She leans up and rubs her face against my cheek. "Mmm, freshly shaved cheeks," she coos.

There is this sweet innocence about Juliette that's totally sexy. Even better, she isn't at all inhibited in the sack. I have to say it's my favorite *juxtapose*.

When I move the shower curtain, I have to stop for a couple of seconds, she takes my breath away. With her head tipped back and the water running suggestively over her body, she looks like an erotic painting.

I stick my finger into the stream of water and pull back. "You like the water a little hot there. You think I can turn it down a bit?" I comment as the heat from the shower overwhelms me.

"Only if you can figure out some other way to keep me warm?" she flirts.

"I'm sure I can figure something out." That's when I notice she only has soap, shampoo and cream rinse. Mariana had so many bottles and containers; our shower was an obstacle course. This is going to be easy, I won't use the wrong product. With the soap all frothed up, I use it as a lubricant and run my hands over all her curves. You can't beat starting your day with some nice clean shower sex.

It's a little tricky having sex in the shower, kind of like Twister. I bend my body and hold onto the plumbing so I don't slip while getting the right leverage to plunge into her. The shower also isn't just a great place for singing. As her gasps and moans echo off the walls, my pace picks up until I revel in the ecstasy of release.

After a quick rinse, I grab one of her towels, handing Juliette the other one. Quickly I dry off, then wrap my towel around my waist and lean against the door. Now I can enjoy watching Juliette towel off, apply body lotion and brush out her hair. She gives me a pointed look.

"Are you enjoying watching me get ready?" she asks.

"Yes. I. Am."

She smiles shyly and shakes her head while she applies stuff to her hair. Then slowly and purposely she stalks over to me. I pull her tight and kiss her long and deep while squeezing her ass. I could devour this woman.

"If we didn't just have sex, I would have you back in the sack for another round," I whisper.

Back in her room, she searches her closet while only wearing underwear. This is why I like being in a relationship. You get to spend time hanging out with a hot woman while they're naked or changing.

"What are we doing today?" she inquires.

"I'm hungry. Let's grab some breakfast, we'll figure out the rest later."

Juliette throws on Lycra pants and shirt. Whoever the designer was who convinced women to wear yoga pants, deserves a medal.

"I need something to drink. We have some juice in the kitchen," she informs me as we leave her bedroom.

While we're in the kitchen, her roommate's boyfriend enters the living room, finds his sneakers, and sits down on the couch to tie them up.

"Good morning," I exclaim.

He looks up, gives a cursory nod as he double-checks the two of us out. He's the kind of guy who broadcasts pure dickishness.

"Friendly guy. I take it he heard us in the shower," I comment to Juliette after he leaves.

"I think that's the friendliest he's ever been."

"Go grab your jacket, I need to eat."

• • • •

WE GRAB A BITE A COUPLE blocks away, then check out the local farmers market, picking up food for lunch and dinner. Arriving back at Juliette's, her roommate Cassie makes a grand appearance. I've only seen her on TV and, of course, the larger than life-size mural plastered across the dining room wall.

Cassie struts into the kitchen, wearing Lycra pants and top, that's so form-fitting, it leaves nothing to my imagination. Real life Cassie has nothing on any picture. She's the most exquisite woman I've ever seen. Her body is perfect. Her face is amazing. Her bone structure is flawless and her porcelain skin looks like it's chiseled out of marble. She exudes sexuality and confidence. I'm floored when she gives me a flirty smile that reeks of pure lust.

"I take it I didn't imagine someone was having sex in your bathroom this morning?" she coos as every atom in her being oozes pheromones.

"I'm Nate," I exclaim as I extending my hand.

She looks at my hand as she raises one eyebrow, "I'm Cassie," she coolly exclaims. Turning her gaze to Juliette she continues, "I have sex-dar; I always know when someone's having sex."

Cassie's breathtakingly beautiful and she has amazing sexual charisma. My college self would be dumping Juliette right now to screw Cassie, because I know she'd let me. But, my adult self has better impulse control. I'm also no longer interested in hooking up, and with someone like Cassie, that's all it would be. What's obvious, is Cassie's manipulative—using sex for control. She definitely is trying to fuck with Juliette's head by flirting with me. Juliette told me they've been best friends since childhood. I wonder what little game Cassie is playing and why Juliette stays around. Can Juliette be that naive?

I make sure Cassie gets the message strong and clear that I'm not interested in any of her games. I pull Juliette in front of me, wrap my arms around Juliette, and broadcast loudly that this little game is not going anywhere.

"Then, your sex-dar must have been on high alert this weekend," I reply, while bending down and kissing the sweet spot between Juliette's shoulder and neck, eliciting a small giggle.

Cassie raises her eyebrows and gives Juliette a sly smile, "I'm making a shake, want some?"

"I'll pass on drinking liquid grass," Juliette replies. I tickle her, she giggles. "Where've you been? I don't think I've seen you since last weekend."

Cassie pulls out a bunch of green things from the refrigerator. "Mostly at Luke's, I've been hanging with a couple of the girlfriends. I'm meeting them at noon for a little pre-game tailgating party."

Tired of Cassie's little game, I pull Juliette out of the kitchen.

"Hey, have you heard from Jack recently?" Cassie calls out.

Juliette stops.

"It was after Thanksgiving, maybe Sunday or Monday."

Cassie is messing with Juliette. Now she's messing with me. Who the hell is Jack? She's talking about him right in front of me for a reason. Is Jack some old boyfriend who's still in the picture? I'm not going to let this fester. As soon as we're in Juliette's room I pull her onto my lap.

"Who's Jack?"

"Cassie's older brother. He's in the army. Knowing him he's doing something ridiculously dangerous. We've been pen pals for years."

"Did you date Jack?"

"Jack?" Juliette responds in surprise. "That would be like dating a brother. We didn't even get along growing up. After he signed up for the Army, I started sending him silly emails. He's had a strained relationship with his parents and Cassie isn't much into writing, so I do my part by keeping him connected to home."

Good, this Jack might have something for Juliette, but she's not interested. Still, I don't understand what game Cassie's playing.

"A hike would be nice. Where can we go?" I ask.

"Rancho's the closest, though I need to warn you, on the weekend, the parking lot is a total zoo. There's a crazy protocol for getting a space. Be prepared to wait ten or fifteen minutes."

"Are you sure you want to go there?"

"It's the best place around."

"Rancho it is."

"You run, right?" she asks as she crawls off my lap.

"Yes."

"How about a trail run instead of a hike? If we get tired, we can turn it into a hike."

"That works, but we'll need to stop at my place so I can get the right gear."

• • • •

JULIETTE DIRECTS ME to Rancho, explaining how you need to idle at the mouth of the parking lot while you wait for a space to open up. About five minutes after we choose a row to idle in, a white SUV idles behind us. It takes another five minutes before two guys walk down the path and get into their car. As the red tail lights on their car come on, the woman idling behind us starts maneuvering her SUV around us.

"Oh, no she doesn't!" Juliette yells.

She darts out of my Jeep and runs right in front of the white SUV, blocking her from the parking space. Now that's the little firecracker I met at Jamie's soccer game. She's been so sweet and shy I forgot how spirited she is.

The guys pull out and Juliette directs me to move into the spot. Parking quickly, I jump out of my Jeep in time to hear Juliette scolding the woman in the white SUV.

"You should know better. Don't cut in line."

I grab a hold of her arm and walk her out of the parking lot.

"Shit, I thought you were going to beat her up," I exclaim, while inside I'm smiling, I like my woman feisty.

"Me? I've never hit anyone. But, that woman really pissed me off. She was waiting behind us, so she knows the protocol. She didn't want to wait her turn. I bet she lives in Los Altos. Los Altos SUV driving women act so entitled."

"I thought you grew up in Los Altos."

"That's how I know."

She's been so sweet, I forget what a little terror she can be.

"Do you act this scrappy at work?"

"Not yet, I'm so junior I haven't yet learned enough of the ropes to say anything."

We start running at an easy pace. As we warm up and feel each other out, our pace picks up. As Juliette picks up the pace again, I realize she doesn't have an off switch, she's going to burn herself out halfway through this run.

"Hey, hotshot, please don't kill yourself out here. You might be only a little bit of a thing but I still don't want to have to carry you back to the car."

"I'm fine," she declares.

"Oh, I know you're fine," I exclaim as I check out her hot ass. "How about you do this for me, run a little slower for me."

Man, it's like soccer with her and the other little terror. She tears into exercise with no thought to her own well-being.

"Juliette, how about you don't kill yourself on the run. I have some ideas of how we can spend the rest of the day and you bonking on a run doesn't fit in."

This last plea actually works as we take the single-track path. She goes first, to pace me and so I get to run with a view of her ass.

• • • •

BACK AT JULIETTE'S apartment, we eat lunch on the living room ottoman as we watch the football game on TV. Cassie's spotlighted again, though I'm not surprised, she's magnificent.

"I don't think I've ever met two people who are as polar opposite as you and Cassie," I comment, when Cassie comes up on the screen.

"Yeah, but our friendship works."

"Until she started flirting and strutting around in front of me this morning. Juliette, I wasn't born yesterday. She heard us in the kitchen; she came strutting out wearing almost nothing, and then she was hitting on me. Come on, when a guy isn't around she doesn't dress and act like that. You weren't very happy with her behavior. I didn't miss that either."

Juliette's brow is knit as I lay out my observation. She leans her face into my hand as I finish up. Cassie might be shockingly beautiful but she doesn't hold a candle to sweet Juliette.

"Don't worry, I wouldn't fuck her with his dick," I console as I point to some random guy on TV. Her eyes get wide from shock, inwardly I chuckle.

At halftime, I pull Juliette into the bathroom. As she undresses, I realize that I don't want a quickie, I want to watch the rest of the game. Then I want to take my time making love to my new girl. As she towels off from our quick shower, I get an even better idea. The picture of her wearing that red shirt is seared into my brain. Even better than seeing her on TV wearing that shirt, I'm going to get her to wear it today as we make out and watch the game.

After presenting my idea, Juliette rolls her eyes, chuckles, and shrugs as she heads into her room to change her top. I sit on the couch waiting for my fantasy girl to appear. She enters the living room. A fantasy turned to real life is great. Who gives a shit about some football game when a girl that looks like this in front of me. Juliette naturally has this sweet way of holding her head, making her look demure. Combined with her rocking body busting out of the sexy shirt, I'm knocked out. I pull her onto my lap, I can't keep my hands off her rack.

"I thought you wanted to wait until after the game?" she giggles.

"This shirt is hot, or should I say you're hot in this shirt." I bury my face into her large, perky breasts.

"What is it with this T-shirt?" she squeals.

Kissing her deeply I finally pull up for air, "I couldn't get you out of my head after I saw you on TV last month. All my fantasies had you wearing this T-shirt."

"You're missing the game," she warns.

"Yeah, well I've never followed these teams, but this shirt." I get an even better idea. "Take off your bra and let me see you braless in the shirt."

"Really?"

Taking matters into my own hands, I pull off her shirt and bra. Damn, her tits are amazing. I palm them and take a suck on one of her nipples. She laughs and pulls away, I hand her the T-shirt to put back on.

She gets a devious look on her face and leaves the room. I wonder what she has in store. She comes back wearing the shirt without a bra but carrying her computer. My eyes are glued to her. How many minutes can I stare at her before I take her?

Deliberately she sets up her computer on the far side of the ottoman from me. "I'm checking e-mail, you can look, but I've decided you can't touch till after the game is over," she declares.

She follows that proclamation up with a flirty smile as she stretches her hands over her head.

"This is going to be a long fourth quarter," I murmur as I look at that hot, tight body and think how sexy she is when she gets all dominatrix on me. From experience I know, I'm not into slapping, tying up or other sadomasochistic sexual activities. It was surprising and hot the first few times, but it's not anything I'd ever seek out. But that still leaves a lot of things I'm interested in doing.

"Wearing that shirt makes me conjure up some really wild things we can do," I pant out, hoping I'm not actually drooling.

"Keep fantasizing over there, buddy," she smirks.

The second the fourth quarter is over I tackle her. Now I get to live some of my fantasies on her roommate's nice soft living room rug.

Monday morning, waking up in Juliette's bed, reality hits me hard, there are five days before the weekend, which is too long. I've read that new relationships have the same effect on your brain as obsessive-compulsive disorder. That sure is the case with me; I obsessively and compulsively want to screw Juliette.

"I don't want to wait till Friday to see you again. Can you work in a late dinner?" I suggest.

"Saturday you said you would be done at two but actually showed up after four. I think you're being way too optimistic to think that you can make it out of work in time for dinner. Why don't we plan on a mid-week booty call?" she replies.

What? Wait! Damn, Juliette is the best girlfriend ever. There has to be a hitch.

"You're cool with a booty call?" I hedge.

"If all I get is a booty call, no, not at all. If you show up drunk at midnight, you're going to get a door slammed in your face. But we spent the entire weekend together. We're both busy. Hopefully, we'll spend next weekend together. If we want to see each other during the work week, we'll need to be happy with a late-night booty call, right?"

"You're way too logical, when does crazy come out?"

"Oh, jumping out of the car and yelling at a woman wasn't crazy enough for you?"

"A guy would do something like that. When do you get all emotionally crazy?"

"Remember this conversation the day before my period. Except if you call me emotionally crazy then, I'll probably eviscerate you."

Shockingly honest, but she makes a good point.

We head out together. Before I leave I pull her in for another long kiss. "This was a very good weekend. I'll text you and we can figure out when I get my booty call."

"Nate, it's my booty call."

Well, hot damn. If we didn't have sex twenty minutes ago, I think I'd be late for work.

We get together on Tuesday.

I'm obsessed with Juliette. I crave her. I push my luck by texting her on Thursday.

Me: *Do I get a booty call tonight?*

Juliette: *Only if I get to choose tonight's position.*

Damn, I almost get a hard-on from reading that text. How am I going to concentrate for the rest of the day knowing what's in store for me tonight?

At Juliette's house, she meets me at the door wearing only a big, soft robe, then with a secret smile sends me off to bed. Now I wonder what she's up to, I strip down, pull my phone and condoms out of my bag and wait for her.

It's easy to tell she hasn't had a lot of varied sexual experiences, but I like her sweet naivety and I have no problem showing her some new moves. I'm curious what she has in mind. As I wait to see what she's going to do, she gets a nervous smile on her face.

Maybe this isn't such a good idea.

Maybe I should take over.

Then her robe falls off her shoulders exposing her rocking naked body. Strutting over to me, she looks insecure and sexy all in one shot. I reach my hand out to bring her close.

"No, this is my turn. You only get to touch me when I tell you to touch me."

Damn, she's my own little sex goddess.

I lean back to enjoy the show.

She proceeds to slowly go down on me. She's so tentative that I don't think she's ever done this before, but I'm not about to stop her since it feels so good and being her first is...thrilling.

For a rookie, I've got to give her credit; she has a lot of natural ability. Before I actually blow, she impales herself on my cock and we're off for an amazing round of sex with her on top. Then again, the word amazing doesn't cut it. Juliette and I have this great natural rhythm. Mariana was wilder in bed, but I don't think we were ever this simpatico.

• • • •

ON SATURDAY, I HEAD to Juliette's to pick her up so we can attend a holiday dinner at my boss's house. When she opens the door she's ready, even to the point of wearing her coat. I'm glad she's being a good sport; then again, I'm going to her holiday party next weekend. I'm sure the guys where she works have seen the pictures of her at the football game and, at least, a few had the same reaction as me. My goal at her party is to make sure those guys know she's taken.

Arriving at my boss's house, we're greeted by his wife. A server takes Juliette's coat and I just about fall over.

Damn!

She looks like Jessica Rabbit and I must look like an idiot cartoon with my eyes popping and my tongue hanging out.

Her hair is up and she's wearing come-fuck-me high heels and a tight little black dress, a huge departure from what she normally wears. She looks amazing, elegant, classy, but sexy as hell. The dress is low-cut showing off her amazing rack, but it has this mesh top, which makes it look like you really shouldn't be seeing her breasts, which makes looking at them even hotter. Now I wonder how I'm going to make it the whole night without touching her.

She's the perfect date too; polite, friendly, and comfortable in this environment. In an attempt to get each of us a drink, I get caught up in shaking hands and hellos with my new colleagues. Being the new guy; I need to make a good impression since I want these guys to work with me. Over my shoulder I glance at Juliette, she's perched on a large ottoman surrounded by the wives. She peers at me from over her shoulder; I get the perfect shot of her slim waist, elegant neck, and beautiful face as our eyes connect and she gives me a secret smile.

Damn, I think I'm in love.

I know I'm in lust.

I smile back, losing track of the conversation. The other doctor follows my gaze. After checking out Juliette, he gives me a knowing nod. He too is impressed by my pretty date. Finally breaking away from him, I bring her the glass of wine I promised ages ago.

After dinner, my boss brings us into his family room and starts talking about last year's accomplishments. With my back against the wall, I pull Juliette into my arms. Man, she's hot. My boss lowers the lights and brings up a video, this gives me a great idea. Silently I grab Juliette by the hand and pull her into the powder room.

"Nate...." is all she gets out as I quickly close the door and block her against the wall.

She pushes me away. "Nate, we can't do this in your boss's bathroom," she whispers in surprise.

"You look so hot, I've spent the entire evening trying to control my hard on. No one's going to miss us," I whisper back. She bites her lip and excitement flashes across her face.

"We cool?" I question.

She nods. That's all I need. I flip her around so we're back to front. She gasps, I pull her dress up to her waist.

"Grab a hold of the sink," I command.

Damn, I've been staring at the white column of her neck; it looks inviting. I lean in and lick it.

"Baby, arch your back," I implore, as I unzip my pants, releasing my hard-on while sliding her panties to the side. I give her clit a rub the way I've learned she likes. My dick screams to be inside of her. After angling myself to get in, I start thrusting. Man, the vision of Juliette in the mirror is awesome. Her boobs look amazing in that see-through part of her top as they jump up and down with each thrust.

"Your tits are so hot," I gasp into her ear as she huffs and squeaks trying to keep her noise down.

My dick is so happy being squeezed by her tight V. Forcing my eyes up at just the right time, I get to see her gasp and her eyes close. Then bliss, as I tighten up with that tingle before I let myself go. I can't keep my eyes off her as she straightens herself up. Man, with that just fucked flush across her cheeks, she's one beautiful woman. When she's ready, I snatch her hand and lead her to the back wall of the family room.

As the lights go up, I silently cheer, I'm one lucky bastard. Hell, even if the other doctors realized we left the room, what are they going to say?

Chapter 10 – Winter Vacation

Christmas arrives; Jamie and I fly down to meet our parents in Mexico. Juliette's gotten under my skin, I realize how much I miss her. I'm waiting until I'm sure Juliette is more than a passing fad, to tell my family about her. After we spend the morning scuba diving, Jamie eyes me as I lay by the pool and catch up on my reading.

"Why are you staring at me?" I question.

"What's up with you? There are obviously some single women at the bar," she exclaims. She points to a group of pretty young women I noticed ages ago. "You haven't hit on any of them."

"I'm no longer that guy, I've grown up."

"No one changes this much. You've got a woman. With the look on your face, I'm right. Damn Nate, you're amazing. You've been in California for less than a month. You're introducing her to me the second we get back."

"Jamie, do you realize you've carried on a whole conversation without me saying a word."

"Don't you play your games with me, Nate. I know you too well. I hope you made a better choice this time."

"You can't give me any shit since you're dating Tyler."

"Tyler is off the table Nate. I want to know about your new woman."

"Actually, you've met her."

"Who Nate, you need to tell me."

"Juliette, the woman you took out at that soccer game."

"I knew something was going on when you helped her off the field."

. . . .

BACK IN TOWN FOR NEW Years, Juliette and I head up to her friend's cabin in Tahoe. At Grass Valley the rain turns to snow, luckily, I still have my snow tires on my 4WD Jeep.

"What is it with these people? They drive like they've never driven in snow before," I complain.

Just then, someone driving too fast for the conditions, fishtails, barely missing me, as they fly past.

"You're probably right. Not too many inclement conditions down in the bay area. They probably have never driven in snow."

A little bit farther the traffic slows for the CalTrans chain control station. I've never driven on a road that required chains. It's probably because people in Western New York and the Midwest know how to drive in snow. My Jeep with its four-wheel drive and snow tires lets me pass through the inspection site. We make good time since most of the cars and trucks on the road have chains and cannot travel any faster than twenty-five as they hug the right lane.

The cabin is actually a three bedroom, three-bath house in a large woodsy subdivision. We park in the driveway and trudge through the snow to the front door. We're greeted by cheers as Juliette friends race to meet us.

"Nate meet Jennifer," Juliette sings out as she introduces me to a petite Asian woman who gives me a little wave. A medium height blond with navy blue eyes is then introduced as Meredith.

From the kitchen, a Latino guy immerges. "Did you really bring more food?"

"Each of us chose a day. I brought Sunday," Juliette explains.

He pulls Meredith into a warm embrace. "By the look of it you ladies have an issue with portion control. There's enough food here for a month."

"Nate, this is Sam, Meredith's boyfriend. He also went to college with us." Juliette explains. "Did you bring Rocket?" she asks Jennifer.

"He ran to the store to get beer."

"Kind of shocking, with all the food you guys brought, no one thought of bringing beer," Sam states.

"Next time we'll let you take care of food," Jennifer responds.

"No way, we've done that before. All we'll get to eat are energy bars and frozen pizza," Juliette replies.

About a half an hour later, a guy around my age enters. He's carrying a couple of cases of beer. He kicks the snow off his boots.

"Safeway's a zoo," he declares. "The shelves are almost empty, and this storm is going to get worse before it gets better."

"I assume you're Rocket." I reach out my hand. "I'm Nate."

"Nate, you're lucky you got up in time, I hear they're closing highway 80."

"What's for dinner?" Sam interrupts.

"I brought your favorite," Meredith coos.

"Steak?" Sam questions.

Meredith gives him a light peck on his cheek. "I know my man."

"I'll get the barbecue going," Sam declares. He pulls on a fleece and reaches for his boots.

"Don't you think it would be easier to use the broiler?" Meredith questions.

"Yeah, but the food tastes better on a grill and I'd like to shovel off the hot tub."

"If he wants to stand out in the cold to grill some steaks, I'm all open for it. It's snowing so hard, keeping the snow off the hot tub will be a Sisyphean effort," Rocket coolly responds from in front of the fireplace.

I join Sam. On the deck, I raise my hands to catch the falling snow; it looks really pretty since there isn't any wind. Sam and I each grab a shovel and uncover the deck, barbecue, and hot tub. We hunker down and watch the steaks cook.

"You a football fan?" Sam asks breaking the silence.

"Yeah, Buffalo."

"Maybe another year...I'm a pseudo-San Francisco fan, but growing up in south Florida, Miami will always be my team."

We stomp our feet and take turns shoveling the snow to keep ourselves warm.

"I've known all the princesses since their freshman year," Sam confides.

He takes one look at my blank face and chuckles under his breath. "This is your first introduction to the princesses. Actually, there are seven of them." Pointing with his chin to the house, "Those three and four more including Isabelle, whose house we're at.

"Yeah, I met Isabelle the day I met Juliette. She's a tiny little thing with a lot of spunk."

"You have no idea," Sam chuckles. "There's also Olivia, Kelly, and Hita. They all attended the Halloween parties as princesses their freshman year."

"...Like the princesses the little preschool girls all dress as?"

"Well, sort of. Though the princesses that showed up at my fraternity party were nothing like what you'd see at a preschool...as in every guy at that party had a princess fantasy that night."

Like my red shirt fantasy? I wonder if Juliette still has her princess costume...and if she's willing to try it on for me? This might make for an interesting evening. When we get inside, I pull Juliette close.

"I heard you were a princess in college," I whisper in her ear.

She barks out a laugh, gives me a sweet kiss on my cheek, and bats her eyes.

"Yeah, I was Snow White."

"I have an evil step-monster," Meredith declares.

"She was Cinderella," Juliette explains,

"Hey, Mulan!" Meredith yells to Jennifer,

"Yeah?"

"Nate found out about our alter egos."

"Jen actually chaperoned at her school Halloween party dressed as Mulan," Rocket volunteers.

"You wore that outfit to your middle school?" Meredith's gasps.

"I made the kimono a lot bigger, sexy Mulan wouldn't go over well with my administration or the parents."

"It's not only us, Sam dressed as Prince Charming?" Juliette teases.

"You were in on it?" Rocket questions.

"It was a ploy to catch Cinderella, and it worked," he declares in defense.

"I never even had to lose a shoe to get him to sweep me off my feet," Meredith demurs. While Jennifer and Juliette pretend to gag.

When dinner is over, we get into a wild game of poker. Another Juliette surprise, she's a good player, though she has a few tells that she broadcasts too loudly. I'm glad that my girl isn't too hard for me to read.

Rocket's an interesting guy. He must be around my age. He's rough around the edges, has muscles that look like they come from hard work, not weight lifting, sports two sleeves of tattoos, but he also must be classically educated and well-read, based on his comments. Now if Jamie was dating this guy, I'd be thrilled.

"I almost forgot," Jennifer squeals after losing again, "One of my students showed me this."

She runs to her room and returns with her computer. She pulls up a YouTube video. It's a song produced in four segments on the screen. The guy did a clever job. It's a takeoff of the princesses, called *After Ever After* starring Cinderella and Mulan.

"Why didn't he include Snow White? She's one of the most important princesses," Juliette pouts.

"Mulan hardly ever gets any coverage. Now you know how I feel." Jennifer teases back.

Right before midnight, we fold up our game and head to the living room to gather around the fireplace. Sam pulls out a bottle of Jägermeister. The women throw pillows at him.

"Not again," they chant.

"Hey, this is a tradition, and if we don't follow through we'll have bad luck."

It turns out Sam's New Year's tradition is to take a mouthful of Jägermeister, spit it into the fire, then state a New Year's wish or resolution. Needless to say, this is a waste of Jägermeister, and quickly turns ridiculous, though it is a lot of fun as we watch the flames leap and sizzle with each mouthful we spit.

At some point, Sam's phone goes off. "Thirty seconds until the New Year," he announces as he pulls Meredith onto his lap. He has the right idea, I too pull Juliette into my arms. Sam holds up his phone as we count down. When it reaches twelve, we all kiss our partner.

After our kiss, it hits me how tired I am and how much I want to break the New Year in by having a tumble with my girl before I fall asleep. With my arms wrapped around Juliette, I stand and carry her off to bed. Though as I start rocking into her, I think the house might shake off its foundation with three young couples, all with the same idea.

• • • •

WHEN I WAKE, THE MORNING light is wrong. Quietly I pull back the window shade, all I see is snow. Either the wind picked up, or we're buried. Juliette is soundly sleeping as I dress and head into the living room. I find Rocket pulling on his boots.

"What are you up to?"

"My dog needs to take a leak," Rocket explains as he picks up a shovel. "Looks like I'll need to dig a path."

I find my warm clothes, grab a shovel and join him in the garage. He opens the garage door. All we see is a wall of white.

"Damn, that's a lot of snow."

He pokes with his shovel at the top of the garage.

"Shit, it's still snowing. I can't tell if this is a snowbank or we have over seven feet."

The two of us pitch in to clear a path from the door as Rocket's dog starts whining loudly.

"Dude, your dog's standing at the door whining."

"She's never seen snow before."

"We've got to make it fun."

He coxes his reluctant dog out of the house while I gently throw her a snowball. She tries to catch it like a ball but becomes totally confused when it breaks apart in her mouth. The two of us scramble out of the garage and over the snow sinking deep as we throw snowballs to his dog. Reluctantly she joins us. After a while, we've got her swimming through the thick snow. It's fun and surprisingly exhausting.

After breakfast, everyone heads outside to unbury my Jeep. Surprisingly it's still snowing. After lunch, it finally stops. We head outside again. I work up a sweat shoveling. With the driveway almost clear, I hear a yell. Turning to the noise, I spot Rocket on the roof. We all turn to watch him. He swan dives off the roof and into the front lawn. He lands in what appears to be an explosion of snow.

"Rocket," Jennifer screams.

"Did he just commit suicide?" Meredith gasps.

His dog goes wild barking.

The spot he dove into, looks like a cartoon. Snow flies in the air and Rocket finally emerges looking like the Abominable Snowman.

"That was amazing. You've got to try it," he laughs and hollers.

"Rocket, I thought you killed yourself," Jennifer rages.

He runs up to Jennifer and picks her up, she squeals really loudly.

"It's like jumping into a snow cone," he rejoices.

"Come on Jen, it was fun."

"I'm a princess, not a policeman," she responds.

"Come on princess, this will be fun."

Jennifer backs up and shakes her head.

"Hell, if she won't do it I will," Juliette mutters from behind me. I turn in time to watch Juliette follow Rocket's path up to the roof.

"Hell yeah," Sam yells from behind me. Before I know it, everyone but Jennifer is on the roof. As a group, we decide to hold hands and on the count of three jump.

"I'll call for help if you idiots brake your necks," Jennifer calls up to us.

"With this amount of snow, even if you get through, no one will be able to get to us." Sam answers.

"Just go for it." Juliette cheers. "On the count of three, I'm jumping."

The landing is soft; it does feel like falling into a giant snow cone. I practically have to swim to get back to the driveway. When I'm almost there, I feel someone pull on the waist of my pants, then I feel cold snow on my butt. Twisting around, I see Juliette's face, beaming.

"Not so smart," I call out. She tries to scramble away. But the snow is so thick it's hard to move. I grab a hold of her. She squeals really loudly.

"What comes around goes around," I sing out as I take a handful of snow and shove it down her back. She squeals again loudly as she tries to scramble away. Needless to say, the next twenty minutes turn into a massive snowball war. Lucky for us the storm doesn't take out the power. Since we're all freezing cold, we head to the hot tub to warm up.

By Sunday, we finally make it to the ski resort. Another pleasant surprise, Juliette's a good skier. While Meredith, Sam, and Jennifer head to the beginner slopes for a lesson, Rocket joins Juliette and me. It turns out he's a proficient and flashy snowboarder.

Meeting Juliette at the horse arena on Saturday afternoon has turned into one of the highlights of my week. Juliette no longer needs to lead my horse back to the stables since I'm learning to ride.

"The movies make riding look easy."

"Nate, you need to think like a horse so you can better predict their behaviors."

"How would I know how a horse thinks?"

"They're grazers. They survive in the wild by being skittish. You need to predict what will spook them before they bolt. Then keep them facing what scares them. Predators don't attack a horse from the front."

Even with everything I need to think about, it's still enjoyable to ride a horse to the stable.

No longer needing anyone to tell me what to do, I pull off Jackson's saddle and start curry combing him.

"Tomorrow should be nice. Do you want to take the horses out for a picnic? You can practice trotting. If you're really good I'll even let you canter," she flirts.

"How is riding a horse sexy?"

"Picnic, blanket on the ground, remote location."

"Cold, hard ground."

"Really? We're that old already?"

I pull her close and kiss that sassy mouth.

"Why wait. Have you ever done it in the hay?"

"It's forty-five degrees. Can't we wait to do it in my nice warm bed?"

"What? We're that old already?"

"Can you figure out how to do it without me getting cold?"

"Baby, that's a challenge I'm up to."

I grab Jackson's blanket and throw it over a couple of bales of hay.

Juliette squeals as I grab her by the waist and hoist her on top.

"I like all that skin, but I think to stay warm I'll pass on it until later," I growl.

I pull her jeans down past her knees and unzip mine. She wraps her hands around my neck.

"Poor Jackson," she snickers. "Doing this in front of a gelding probably makes him feel jealous."

"I think he has a thing for me, but we're not going there."

She lets out a squeal as I thrust into her. Man, she feels good.

. . . .

JAMIE INVITES JULIETTE and me over for dinner, of course, Tyler's there. Dinner goes well. Jamie and Juliette hit it off. I can tell Jamie really likes her.

"Why were you so rude to Tyler?" Juliette questions on the drive home.

"What does my sister see in him?"

"I get it. He has this edgy surfer boy casual thing going. It's kind of sexy."

"You think Tyler's sexy?"

"I didn't say I think he's sexy. But he has this casual, outdoorsy, wild boy thing going which some women find sexy. More than that, from what Jamie said, her office is a total shark tank. I can see that at the end of the day, it's relaxing for her to come home to someone like him."

"You think a loser is someone she should come home to?"

"Listen to yourself; you're so harsh on Tyler. This is your sister, you need to be more supportive. If not, you will drive a big wedge in your relationship. Anyways how many successful, competitive men choose a nice, sweet woman who has no interest in having a career?"

"It's not the same thing."

"It's exactly the same thing."

"Stay at home moms aren't losers."

"Stay at home moms work really hard," Juliette replies. "You're misconstruing what I'm saying. What I'm saying is, you choose a partner who reflects how you want to spend your downtime. For me, I'm athletic, I choose a guy who likes to work out. Jamie works in a really competitive space. When she comes home, she wants someone who is mellow, no pressure, and appreciates everything she does."

"She can choose a mellow guy who's not a pot head looser?"

"Nate, you need to embrace who she chooses. What would you do if she hated me? Would you break up with me or would you avoid Jamie?"

"Jamie likes you."

"Come on, you know what I'm getting at."

I can vividly remember Jamie complaining about Mariana and me giving Jamie an ultimatum.

Juliette rubs my shoulder. "I know Ty rubs you the wrong way but you need to look at the bigger picture. If this is who Jamie needs in her life to be happy, you need to learn how to be supportive."

• • • •

ON MY ROUNDS, I HEAD into one of my patient's room. He's a thirty-seven-year-old competitive tennis player with a new hip. As I'm examining him, his physical therapist comes in followed by a posse of trainees, the benefit or downside of getting medical treatment at a teaching hospital. The lead physical therapist waits until I'm done. He introduces himself to the patient. I get a prickle at the back of my neck as I briefly listen to what he's saying before I take off.

As I look around my eyes land on Mariana.

What the fuck?

How can this be?

I look again, wondering if this is a mirage.

No, it's Mariana.

I can tell she's as shocked to see me as I am to see her. Our eyes lock. I stand there staring.

Unable to move.

Unable to speak.

It's been sixteen months.

I finally pull myself together enough to leave the room. My heart races as I head down the hall, wondering if I had a hallucination.

"Nate," the sound of my name with that inflection no one else can replicate reverberates off the walls of the hallway.

Do I stop?

Do I continue?

Do I search for closure?

My chest constricts.

I slowly turn around.

She approaches in that half run she does that has always turned me on.

"Nate...." Her bottom lip quivers, "I miss you."

What!

"You don't get to take off without a word and then say that."

She purses her lips, reaches her hand out and strokes my arm. I flinch from the touch while my damn dick twitches. I take a step back. My broken heart, that had finally healed, starts to bleed.

Does this woman still have control over me?

Instead of doing the smart thing, turning and running away from her as fast as I can, I stand glued to the floor.

"What are you doing here?"

"Getting a certification. What are you doing here?"

I take another step back, "I live here now."

"Please, let's at least talk."

"What could we possibly talk about?" I shake my head, turn, and walk away. My head is so not in the game as I blindly make my way outside. I text the attending I'm working with and tell him I'm running late. My heart is beating a million miles an hour as I take a long walk around campus. Nothing comes to me. For months I fantasized about running into Mariana again. At first, I was magnanimous, letting her come back. Then I moved to anger, telling her to go to hell. Now...all I feel is confusion.

She looks the same.

Which is too damn good.

• • • •

JULIETTE AND I DON'T have plans to get together tonight but I need to see her, touch her, and screw her. I need to get Mariana out of my head. That voice, I had suppressed that amazing melodic voice of hers. Now all I can hear is that voice in my head.

Nate: *Booty call after hockey?*

Juliette: *You taking new vitamins?*

Nate: *My bed's cold*

Juliette: *How romantic – I'll buy you a bed warmer*

Nate: *You're my bed warmer*

Juliette: *Don't ring the bell*

Man, that woman's just too easy...and I'm complaining about that?

At hockey practice, I'm a total raging bear on the ice. One of the guys checks me against the boards, pushing me hard.

"Dude, this isn't college," he growls into my ear, "We're a bunch of old guys who need to go to work tomorrow."

I show up at Juliette's late, way too late to be respectable. I crawl into her warm bed. She's fast asleep. I need to touch her, to reaffirm. I pull her sleeping body close. She snuggles into me.

"I thought old guys needed a couple days off," she murmurs,

"Yeah, when I'm an old guy, I'll need a couple of days off. Anyway, you're wearing too many clothes. I want skin."

She groans as she strips off her T and pajama pants.

"What I do for you."

She tilts her head up and gives me a light kiss. My fingers ache to feel all that nice, sweet skin. I move closer so our lips are tight, my fingers feeling her curves, and my dick twitches and screaming for release. My nose fills with the smell of Juliette while I listen to her gasps. Thrusting into her, the surge and release feel just too good. Real...Right... Damn, I'm glad I'm here with her tonight.

• • • •

I FIND OUT THAT MARIANA'S here for three months, working in the same ward as me. I know we'll run into each other again. I take it out in the gym. I'm back to being a holy terror on the bag. I've got a great girl, and we're happy. Why does running into Mariana throw me?

I manage to avoid running into Mariana for a few days, mostly because I avoid rounds at the hospital. That plan can last for just so long.

On a day I head in really early for rounds, I spot her walking down the hall. Should I be a coward and duck into the first room? Man up. I take a deep breath, nod, and continue down the hall. That went well. About ten minutes later, my phone beeps. It's a number I recognize but was deleted from my phone.

Unknown: *Lunch? We can talk it out and get over the awkwardness*

I stare at the text. One side of me wants to hear her side of things. The other side screams at me to stay away. I ignore her message. Three months with her here. How will I survive?

The texts continue: *Nate, let's be adults and talk.*

Fuck that. Sixteen months ago, she couldn't return one of my texts. Now I'm immature for not returning hers? What disturbs me the most is what my body does when she's around. How can I be so angry with her and so turned on? How can I care so much for Juliette and still think about Mariana?

I know what I want, things are good with Juliette; I'm not going to blow it.

• • • •

FEBRUARY ARRIVES; I take Juliette to Tahoe for her birthday. The next weekend she tells me we're going to San Francisco to celebrate the Chinese New Year. Juliette and her friends all treat this as a big deal. We drive up with Meredith and Sam. I listen to the three of them talk.

"This is Jennifer's big deal," Meredith explains to me.

"I hope someone warned Rocket. He better act really pleased. Jennifer goes out of her way to celebrate the Chinese New Year."

"Do you remember the guy she dated who afterward said, 'I still don't get what the big deal is. Why'd we have to go to San Francisco for Chinese food and to watch a bunch of high school bands in a parade?" Meredith mocks.

"Dude was totally eviscerated," Sam fills in.

"This is so much fun. I love having all the princesses together." Juliette cheers.

"You guys get together all the time," Sam moans.

"But not in the city, doing something special," Juliette explains.

The night is fun. We all meet at a Chinese restaurant and eat a special meal. Afterward, we head to China Town to watch the parade. Though I can see what the former boyfriend meant. It was fun, but it wasn't mind-blowing. Since I don't want to get eviscerated, I go out of my way to tell Jennifer and Juliette what a great night I'm having. As we drive back home, I reflect, it's nice to have a girlfriend with roots in the area. I don't think I would have ever had any of these experiences if I was on my own.

• • • •

AT THE HOSPITAL, I'M in the men's room washing up.

"Nate, you can't continue to avoid me. At some point, we need to talk," Mariana's melodic voice rings out.

I jump, she's leaning against the door.

"You realize you're in a guy's bathroom."

"Pfff," she replies in that magical way of hers.

"Mariana, I'm done. You take off without a word and now you want to talk?"

"I was in a bad way. I needed some air."

"Good for you. Now can you remove yourself from the door so I can go back to my patients?"

"Nate, just one lunch."

"Fine, you want to talk. Talk here."

"I made a big mistake," she breathes out as she takes a step closer to me. "I'm sorry," she moans as she takes another step, "I miss you." One more step. "Let's try it again?"

In the meantime, I've taken several steps back. I'm now against the wall and she's near. Too near. My body hums from her proximity.

"I would have loved to hear those words sixteen months ago, but I've moved on."

"Another woman? Pfff, it can't be what we had. Please, I want you," she sings out in that sexy voice of hers.

"Mariana," I shake my head, "No."

She moves a little closer, invading my space, running her fingers down my chest. "I know you, you're lying. I can tell, you still want me."

I brush past her. My heart is beating like I've just run a marathon.

. . . .

I WAKE AT THREE IN the morning, Mariana's voice ringing in my ears. Do I still want her? I lie in bed. Reality hits me. I have a choice. Juliette's great, but she's not my wife. We've only been going out for four months. I can break up with her and get back with Mariana.

Is that what I want?

Now I really can't sleep. I climb out of bed, open my top drawer and fish around. Yeah, there, in the back—I pull out the small jewelry box—Mariana's engagement ring. I roll it between my fingers. I should have sent it back to my parents or given it to Jamie. Why did I keep it?

Juliette's sister, who lives in New York City, gets engaged. In February she flies to California. Her parents host a family dinner on Friday night so that we can meet Leigh's fiancé.

Cassie and Juliette can get on a roll telling stories about how difficult her sister Leigh is. Then again, all their stories include the nasty things they did to Leigh when they retaliated, it's not like one sister was an angel and the other was a devil.

"What I'm really looking forward to is meeting the man that would willingly live with Leigh," Juliette declares as we drive to her parents.

"She can't be that bad."

"Nate, she's one of those people who wins by throwing everyone else off."

"Juliette, you and your mother are always texting her. Why do you communicate with her if she's so evil?"

"She's still my sister...and I can control her evil when it's text."

"Leigh, welcome home, congratulations." Juliette sings out as she runs up and throws her arms around a dark-haired woman.

"I see you're still dressing like a college student. You need to dress less dowdy," Leigh responds.

"This isn't *Downton Abby,* I'm not dressing for dinner at home with Mom and Dad," Juliette flippantly replies.

Leigh is unmistakably Juliette's sister. She's taller and thinner, with high cheekbones and hollowed cheeks, though this most likely is due to her being so gaunt. Leigh has her father's blue eyes and her mother's straight dark hair, but they both have the same fine features and that beautiful, pale skin. Leigh reeks of wealth and fashion. She holds herself like a ballerina. What is strikingly different is the energy they each exude. Whereas Juliette comes across sweet and demure, Leigh is haughty, arrogant, and condescending.

"Hi, I'm Leigh's sister, Juliette," she says to an average height, average build, balding guy in his forties,

"This is John," Leigh gushes.

John in turn dismissively acknowledges us.

"Leigh, this is my boyfriend Nate."

"Yes, I gathered."

If Juliette is twenty-five and her sister is two years older, this guy has to be at least twenty years older than Leigh. Juliette said her parents met him once when they visited Leigh in New York.

"Juliette you're here," her mom says as she bustles into the room with glasses and a wine bottle. "Leigh, did you meet Nate? Did everyone have a chance to introduce?"

"Where's dad?" Juliette asks.

"Getting your grandmother, he should be here shortly."

"Did you go on a hike with Mom and Dad this morning?" Juliette asks.

"John and I stayed at the Four Seasons in San Francisco last night. We met friends of John's for lunch."

"John, are you in high tech?" Juliette asks.

"Finance."

"Are you a VC?"

"No."

This is going to be a long dinner.

"John's so modest; he runs this really big fund. All these big names on Wall Street always want to meet with him," Leigh starts gushing.

That explains why some average guy in his forties attracted a stunning woman in her twenties, though I wouldn't say the guy's modest. It's obvious that he's decided none of us are important, what with his dismissive attitude and one-word answers.

The stilted air is broken by Juliette's dad arriving with her grandmother. As they enter the living room Leigh runs up and gives him a great big hug.

"Leigh aren't you going to introduce me to your fiancé," her grandmother scolds.

"Grandma, this is John. John my grandmother Shirley Cole."

"Call me Shirley," she says as she takes a commanding seat on the couch and Juliette's mom hands her a glass of wine. "John, I hear you're in finance in New York City. Were you one of those fellows that brought down the economy back in 2008?"

"It's much more complicated than you're making it out to be," he responds.

"Oh, that's what you finance guys like to say to us seniors when you're stealing all our money." Shirley turns to Leigh, "Leigh sweetheart, you don't want to marry him if he's a crook." Then she points to me. "Now, Nate's a doctor. Nate, did I tell you about my friend Betty's latest surgery?"

"Grandma," Juliette interrupts. "No one wants to hear about your friend's medical problems, and Nate doesn't work on old people, only athletes."

"Mom," Juliette's dad interrupts. "Don't interrogate Nate. We're here to meet John and celebrate the engagement."

"Leigh, you need to show me your engagement ring," Juliette jumps in asking.

This elicits the first smile from Leigh as she lifts her hand and shows off a huge rock; the stone must be five karats.

"How can you even lift your hand? That ring's huge. Aren't you afraid of losing it?" Juliette gushes.

Leigh coyly smiles.

"Leigh, have you decided where you're going to have the wedding?" Juliette's mom asks.

"Well, not here. Of course, it will be in Manhattan."

"One of my friends had money with Bernie Madoff." Shirley states. "Her sister lives in Manhattan and told her he was safe and conservative. Nothing, she's left with nothing. Now he was a great big financial crook." Turning to John she asks, "You're not like Bernie Madoff?"

"Grandma," Leigh gasps. "I bring my fiancé here to meet my family and you call him a crook. You owe John a big apology."

"Well, John, are you a crook like Bernie Madoff?"

It's obvious that John is not taking the crazy grandmother seriously; he seems more bored than anything, as he looks out the window.

This sets the stage for the rest of the dinner as John remains annoyed that he's here, Leigh goes from bored to annoyed, and Shirley moves back to asking me medical questions.

• • • •

"I CAN'T BELIEVE THAT Leigh chose a guy like John. This is a complete disaster," Juliette moans on the way home.

"What are you talking about? John is a smart guy, he has a good job."

"That's how you measure people?"

"Okay, he's a total prick, but so is your sister."

"I was hoping she would marry someone warm and friendly. I figured if she chooses a nice guy, he would mellow her out. I think Leigh and John feed off of each other. He amplifies her worse traits."

"Didn't we just have this conversation in reverse about my sister?"

"I'll give you that neither of us like who our sister has chosen. The difference is, I'm voicing my opinion to you. Since my sister has never asked me my opinion, I smile and suck it in for her. While you voice an opinion that was never asked for."

"She's my sister, I need to set her straight."

"That's where we differ. I believe I need to support my sister's decisions because unsolicited advice is never appreciated. More than that, it's important for me to be part of my sister's life. I'm not going to say or do anything that can be construed as alienating."

We drive the remaining blocks in silence as I digest what Juliette just said. Maybe I should take this as a lesson on how to deal with Jamie.

•••

JAMIE: *Dinner, you and me.*

Me: *What's up?*

Jamie: *I need to talk to my brother.*

Good, maybe she's breaking up with Tyler. I've been trying to take Juliette's advice. I've been going out of my way to be civil to Tyler. I've stopped saying anything negative about him to Jamie. Even so, I would be happy if she dumped him.

We meet. I can tell she has something on her mind. I make sure she's had a beer and some food before I broach the subject.

"What's up?" I finally ask.

"Melissa called me," Jamie replies.

"Really? What's with that?"

"She told me she saw on Facebook that Mariana is in Palo Alto. What's going on Nate? Have you seen her?"

"Nothing's going on. I'm still with Juliette."

"Still?"

"Mariana wants me back."

"What! Please tell me you're not thinking of doing that."

"We were engaged. I love her."

"Love her, not loved her? Shit, Nate. Does Juliette know?"

"Of course not."

"Oh, that sneaky little bitch. Yeah, big coincidence, she shows up at the same hospital as you, just when you finally move on and are happy with a new girl."

"How would she know?"

"Really? I saw the pictures you posted when you were in Tahoe. Anyway, you have lots of mutual friends in Rochester."

Shit, now I'm really glad I hardly ever post anything on Facebook. We sit in silence for a few minutes.

"Is Mariana stalking me? Why?"

"Really, I have to answer that question. You need to tell Juliette."

"Juliette doesn't need to know."

"And when Mariana introduces herself to Juliette and tells her about the two of you working together. How do you think sweet Juliette will take that?"

"Shit, you think Mariana would blow up my relationship?"

"You just said you are in love with her."

"It's complicated. But why would she blow up my relationship?"

"Because you'll be free to go back to her."

"Shit!"

"You wouldn't consider going back to her, right?"

I shake my head.

Shit.

What do I want?

"Nate, think about it," Jamie implores. "What if Juliette's old love was blowing up her phone and she didn't tell you he was back in town. What would you think?"

"How do you know she's blowing up my phone?"

"Really? That psycho. You know if you go back to her, she'll do it again. You'll think everything is wonderful and without notice, she'll leave, again. I bet she did that with her last boyfriend. People have a very consistent MO."

"I didn't say I was going back to Mariana. Things are good with Juliette."

"Keep saying that. Juliette is good for you. You're a happier person with Juliette then you ever were when you were with Mariana. More than that, we get along a lot better since you've been with Juliette."

As I drive home, I debate what to tell Juliette. Jamie's right. If I found out her old boyfriend was in town, she saw him and didn't tell me, I would assume...I would assume exactly what I'm thinking. The old Clash song plays in my brain. *"Should I stay or should I go now? If I go there will be trouble if I stay it will be double...."*

Chapter 13 - Friends

I've run into Cassie's boyfriend, Luke, at Juliette's place, at least fifteen times and the guy still doesn't ever give me more than a disinterested nod. I'm not looking for a new best friend, but he's such a dismissive ass, it's actually weird. Not surprisingly, Luke shows up at work to deal with an injury.

"I'm Dr. Lombard, though we already know each other."

"Were you here last year for my surgery?" Luke questions.

"No, our girlfriends are roommates."

"Oh, yeah, I thought I had seen you before."

Now I'm wondering if he has neurological problems or Prosopagnosia. I'll have to talk to the attending about testing for it. Then again it could be his personality. He's even a dismissive ass to Cassie. But, it's none of my business as long as he doesn't cross the line. I've seen some of his interviews, they shine a camera on the guy and he all of a sudden shows charm and personality. Though I have to admit, he has a very photogenic face and maintains the kind of profile company's love.

• • • •

I NEVER WIND UP TALKING with the attending. Three days later, I'm sitting on the couch checking my messages as I wait for Juliette. Luke comes in and sits down across from me.

"Hey, Nate, I've been doing the standard RICE treatment for my muscle contusions." Grabbing a hold of his thigh, he continues, "The ACL feels like it's holding but I'm not sure if the leg injury is past contusions and actually has some tears."

I guess my first take was correct; he's an arrogant prick who didn't think I was important enough to remember. Even so, I talk him through what he's feeling and see how restricted his movement is. This turns into a regular gig. I'm now starting to wonder if he and Cassie are showing up at Juliette's place more often so Luke can talk about his injuries and postseason training schedule with me.

• • • •

AFTER MY DINNER WITH Jamie, I've become plagued with doubt. Should I tell Juliette?

When did I become this much of a wuss?

Why can't I tell Mariana to fuck off?

Why is she still in my head?

• • • •

AT THE HOSPITAL, I find myself running into Mariana way too often. She's all friendly and sexy. Juliette is great, but Mariana...she gets my blood rolling. But Juliette, we have so much fun together. We like doing the same things; she's easy and friendly, considerate, and practical. Juliette is like a stroll on the beach while Mariana is the biggest, baddest rollercoaster. My brain wants the stroll on the beach while my dick wants the rollercoaster.

At the hospital, as I prep for surgery, alone in a semi-dark room reviewing my patient's images, I hear the door open. I smell her, as I slowly turn around Mariana closes the door. She looks at me with that steamy smile that registers right to my dick.

"I'm busy. Not a good time." I look back at the images.

"Nate...coração."

My chest constricts as my dick twitches from the sound of that voice. She moves closer and places her hand on my shoulder.

I roll away and shake my head. "Mariana, it was over when you left a note on a script pad in our kitchen."

She moves closer, damn, how do I continually let her box me in? She places both hands on my shoulders, leans in, plants a warm, sensual kiss on my lips. At first, my entire body stills. Then my entire nervous system buzzes as my lips respond. I get into it for about twenty seconds, finally, my brain kicks in. I grab her wrists and move her away from me.

"Mariana...shit."

I get up and leave. As I walk down the hall, chills run down my spine. I want her so damn bad.

• • • •

CHRIS, MY CHILDHOOD friend's hockey team is playing the Sharks. I make sure to get tickets for his game. This time, he's not flying out until the next morning. We make plans to meet up at his hotel. Juliette joins me. She's fun to take to a game since she gets into it and asks good questions, mostly about strategy.

"Do I root for our team or Chris's?" Juliette asks as we take our seats at the Shark Tank.

"You root for our team unless Chris has a good play. Then you root for Chris."

The attending sitting next to me talks mostly about the guys that are his patients. I've worked with him a few times and have met some of the players. The game is fun. Chris still looks strong. But they play him like a veteran, to anchor the young guys.

Afterward, Juliette and I head to Chris's hotel to meet up with him at the bar.

Chris joins us. I can't help but notice he's limping. We fist bump, then guy hug. I introduce him to Juliette.

"What's going on? You look strong on the ice."

"This is a young man's sport," he explains as he applies an ice pack on his leg. "All these years of being checked into the boards has taken its toll. I'll work it out more after we talk."

"How're your boys?"

"The boys are good—three and five." He pulls out his phone and shows me some pictures. "Stacey's taking me to the cleaners. Man, I should have waited to get married. The travel schedule, I'm gone the whole season. It's too hard on a marriage. You know too many distractions."

"Yeah, but you've made a lot."

"But, these are my big earning years. Once I retire...." he shakes his head. "I'm looking into my next act. Dude, I only have a GED. I was too busy playing hockey to attend classes."

"Have you thought of what you'll do next?"

"I have investments. Half the investments I had before.... But, I'm thinking of going back to school. I'd like to become a trainer. With all my injuries, I've learned a lot. But enough about me, how's it being a doctor."

"I might have passed my boards, but I still have a year and a half left to my fellowship."

"Yeah, I'm now the old man getting ready to retire and you're the young guy starting out. Funny how at the same age we can be in such different places in our lives."

On the way home, I think about roads not traveled and the choices we make.

* * * *

THE NEXT DAY, AFTER our run, Juliette looks at her phone and turns it so I can see.

"Who is Mariana Castro and why does she want to talk to me about you?"

"What?" I feel my body stiffen and a cold chill run down my spine.

"Mariana Castro left me a message on Facebook messenger. *Can we meet in Palo Alto to talk about Nate?* Do you know who she is and why she's contacting me?"

"Mariana's my old girlfriend."

"The one from Minnesota? The one you lived with?"

I slowly nod my head.

"She's in town?"

I nod again.

"...and you've known about this?"

I nod my head again.

She gasps.

"It's not what you think."

"Have you seen her?"

I nod.

"Have you slept with her?"

"No!" I emphatically pronounce.

"Are you going to tell me what's going on?"

"Nothing's going on. She showed up, that's it."

Juliette's voice gets low as I see the blood run out of her face, "And you didn't tell me about her because...?"

"There's nothing to tell."

"If there's nothing going on why didn't you say something?"

"If your old boyfriend, the one you lived with in London showed up, what would you say?"

"I don't know."

"What would you do?"

"Run in the other direction."

"What would you do if he chased after you? Said he was sorry, that he wanted you back?"

She gasps.

"Wow, what a fantasy. First, I'd enjoy getting that level of satisfaction—you know closure. But, I'd never go back. I don't want him in my life. I don't even want him in the same town. That story is over."

"Yeah, the same for me."

"But why didn't you say anything?"

"Because that story is over."

"But it's not. She's texting me. How did she even know who I am? What did you say?"

"Nothing, I'm not talking to her. I ran into her, she texted me. I swear. You can check my phone, my Facebook account, anything that you need to feel comfortable. I've never replied to her."

"I'm not responding. Will she start doing weird stalky things?'

I shake my head as I wonder how far Mariana is going to go.

. . . .

AFTER OUR CONVERSATION about Mariana, my mind spins. But then it lands. For the first time, when it comes to Mariana, I stop thinking with my dick. I look at my life, what I want. What I really want. What will really make me happy. I know I have a choice and I know this is my future.

The next day I stop at Jamie's. She answers the door.

"What's up?"

I hand her the small velvet box as I enter and sit down on her sofa. She follows me, frowns at the box, and then opens it up.

"An engagement ring? You've only been seeing Juliette for what six months. Don't you think you're going to freak her out if you propose so soon?"

"It's not for Juliette."

"For me? Oh, Nate, have you turned into Caligula?"

"Oh gross, don't even say shit like that out loud."

"Was this Marianna's ring?"

"Yeah, it was grandma's diamond. I think you should have it. I'd never give it to anyone else."

"So you and Marianna?"

"That was over a long time ago."

"Do you still love her?"

"A piece of me will always love her. But, she's not my future. I don't want that ring. I've moved on."

. . . .

A FEW DAYS LATER JULIETTE approaches me all serious,

"I've now received four messages from her. Does she text you?"

"Yeah, she spends way too much time blowing up my phone."

Juliette covers her mouth with her hand and gasps.

Shit, I was afraid of this, she's been dwelling on Marianna. I move close and tip her chin up with my finger. "Juliette, I don't engage with her. I don't respond. I'm not going to lie, when she first came back, I thought about her. But you said it best. Having someone dump you then want you back, it was a fantasy, closure. But Mariana and I are over. We were over a long time ago. She's now provided me with a choice. She's not who I want to be with. I chose you." Juliette slowly nods. I pull her into my arms. "You're who I want."

• • • •

JULIETTE: *Big News Cassie broke up with Luke and is now dating Ford.*

Why do I care and who is Ford? But then I check my schedule to make sure I'm not seeing Luke this week, since I really don't need that kind of drama.

When I stop by Juliette's later that night there's some guy hanging out in front. I'm thinking it's another one of Cassie's stalkers as I puff out my chest.

"Hey, dude," I call out. "Move on, this isn't cool."

"This is a public road, I can stand here if I want," the guy responds.

"Not if you're some dickhead stalker you can't."

"I'm not a stalker, I'm paparazzi. See, I have a camera," he holds his camera up to show me.

"Are you fucking kidding me?"

"No, dude, it's all over the Internet. Ford stole Luke Tomlin's girlfriend. There was this big fight. Tomlin decked him. I'm going to get some pictures. This is the girlfriend's house."

"Dude, I doubt they're hanging out here."

But then I figure this is none of my business. When I enter, I find Juliette in her room.

"Where's Cassie?"

"She took off."

"Do you know there's some idiot outside wanting a picture of her and Ford?"

"I'm not surprised. Cassie's not around. She wanted to make sure she got the well-connected Paparazzi to take her picture, so she and Ford went down to LA."

"Did Tomlin deck the guy?"

"Is that what they're now saying? Cassie's been working overtime to come up with a story the media would be interested in."

"I don't think Tomlin will be too happy to have Cassie telling folks he decked Ford."

"I don't think Cassie cares what Luke thinks. As long as she gets her picture splayed across the media, she'll be happy. Oh, wow, she sent all these naked pictures to Luke. She'll be thrilled if he releases them in retaliation."

"Don't you think that sounds insane?"

"Don't you think that sounds like Cassie."

"And tell me again why the two of you are still friends?"

"Don't you have childhood friends you still are in touch with?"

"Yes, but Cassie...she's rather self-absorbed to the point of being completely narcissistic. I might know guys like that, but I'd never lived with a guy like that."

"We've been friends our whole lives."

What I like about Juliette is her honest naivety and loyalty. She always wants to see the best in people. It's also her Achilles' heel.

"Why don't you stay at my place. At least until that guy out front decides to get someone else's picture. I don't feel comfortable having you here with Cassie chasing weirdo's around."

• • • •

AS I SCRUB IN FOR SURGERY, Mariana comes into the room.

"Mariana, it's over. Stop trying to meet up with my girlfriend, stop blowing up my phone, stop following me, stop coming on to me. I'm done. You moved on once. Move on again."

Mariana dramatically gasps, tears spontaneously run down her cheeks.

I leave.

A few days later when I'm filling out some paperwork, she comes up to me.

I turn in my chair, get up, and leave.

"Wait, Nate," she calls after me.

I don't stop, I don't pause, I keep walking.

A few days later, she approaches me again.

"Do I need to get a restraining order?"

Her eyes get big and wide, she gasps. Her face collapses in sadness as she shakes her head.

"No," she says as she sniffles.

"We have nothing to talk about. Whatever your reasons were for leaving, no longer have anything to do with me. You need to talk to a shrink because I'm not doing this."

I walk away.

One side of me is sad, really sad, but another side is relieved. I hear Juliette's sweet voice in my head; *What a fantasy. First, I'd enjoy getting that level of satisfaction, you know closure. But I'd never go back.*

Juliette's right. I've got to live out a number of fantasies. But Mariana was my past. I want to live in my future.

· · · ·

JULIETTE INFORMS ME that Ford is Bradford Perry, the rock star. The good news is we're saved from Cassie's loud sex for a month when she joins Ford on tour.

A month later, Ford and Cassie show up and spend an inordinate amount of time around the house. In response, Juliette spends a lot of nights at my place, which I like. Neither of us wants to put up with all of Cassie's screaming; which makes me wonder how Ford puts up with it. Cassie's unbelievably hot, but all that screaming in my ear would get old quickly.

I'm over at Juliette's enough to actually witness Ford creating a bunch of new songs. Ford sits down near me with his guitar as I wait for Juliette to gather her stuff.

"Hey, Nate, what do you think of this melody?"

"Ford, asking me what I think...?" I shake my head and laugh, "Dude, ask me about an injury, hockey or MMA, but music? I think you got the wrong guy."

"Nate, my audience doesn't have a degree in music. Does the song stay with you or are you wishing you could change the channel?"

It's interesting to witness the songs evolve. After a while, I can actually give some form of constructive feedback. While I wait for Juliette to get her things together, I sit on the couch and listen.

"Ford, now that sounds good."

"If I ever mess up my hips or knees, I'll call you," Ford chuckles, "Don't guitarists mess up their elbows?"

"Dude, you should see the shit they have me do on the stage."

• • • •

AFTER POLISHING UP a bunch of new songs, he invites us to a private show in San Francisco, where he's trying his new songs out on a live audience. It turns into an amazing evening. It's actually at Bimbo's, a well-known supper club. There are about two hundred people in the audience. Most of them I assume are big wigs in the industry, others are friends of Ford. We are seated with Cassie and Ford's brother. I've hung with Ford for the last couple of months. He's easy to talk to and unassuming in Juliette's living room.

Ford gets up on stage and glows with charisma. It feels like a total transformation from the guy I've been hanging with. What blows my mind is the level of energy I get from this live performance. All the songs he plays are songs I've heard a number of times. On stage, with a band, the songs are in a different league, they're amazing. And Ford's stage presence is awesome; his energy runs through my veins. After about three songs, Ford pulls Cassie up on the stage. He wraps his arm around her.

"My beautiful girlfriend Cassie is going to star in my next music video."

He then dedicates the next song to her as she basks in all the attention.

Juliette taps my arm. "Now, this is the right guy for Cassie."

• • • •

MELISSA AND DAVE, MY former medical school roommates, have a son. I've been chosen as his godfather. Juliette and I fly to New York for the christening, we take the red eye. Juliette arranges for us stay at her sister's. They live on the fortieth floor of a large, meticulously decorated, modern condo, with floor to ceiling windows and amazing views. We arrive at her sisters at nine in the morning; we're let in by a housekeeper. Leigh and John are nowhere to be seen. Though Leigh does leave Juliette detailed instructions on where to get her bridesmaid dress fitted.

Melissa and Dave are now attending doctors and have bought a townhouse in Brooklyn. After Juliette's fitting, we get some deli food to go, then head to their place. For me, it's always comfortable being around them. Juliette fits right in. She is easy going, friendly, and all excited about the new baby. She and Mellissa hit it off as the two of them chat away. This makes for an enjoyable afternoon.

When Juliette gets up to go to the bathroom, Melissa gives me one of her approving looks.

"Now this is the right woman for you."

With a nod at Melissa, I realize that I, too, want Juliette to be my future though I don't yet think she's ready for that conversation. There's no big rush, I still have over a year remaining on my fellowship. I figure once Cassie gets Ford to buy a place in San Francisco, Juliette will need a new roommate and I'll get her to move in with me.

After dinner, I take Juliette up to the top of the Empire State building. I wrap my arms around her and give her a kiss; when we end our kiss she leans with her head on my chest as we stare at all the buildings with their lights on.

"Nice View," I comment.

"Did your sister tell you to do this?"

"What?" I feign in innocence.

Juliette tips up her head, with a smile on her lips she gives me a light kiss before resting her head back on my chest.

I have no idea who Nora Ephron is, I've never seen Sleepless in Seattle, and I would never watch the Mindy Project. But Jamie was right; this is the most romantic place to end a date.

Epilog

***Two years later ***

"THIS IS MY FAVORITE time of day," Juliette declares as we ride back to the stables in the early evening.

When we reach a crossroad, I point west. "We've got time before we lose all our light. Will you indulge me? We can stop at the big live oak. It's my favorite place to watch the sunset."

"I'll race you," she yells as she takes off. I race after her in hot pursuit. The wind's in my hair and the sound of the horse's hoofs pounding the earth fills my ears. Of course, Juliette gets there first.

"I love racing when my size and experience is an asset," she cheers.

I get off my horse and walk to the location that has the perfect view.

"Nate, what are you doing?"

"Come on down, share the sunset with me."

She takes hold of her horse's reins and walks to where I'm standing.

"Nice view."

"Yeah, I love this spot."

She has a satisfied smile as she leans her head against her horse's neck. My chest constricts from nerves, but this is what I want. With a deep breath, I get down on one knee. She looks suspiciously at me.

"Nate?"

Tugging at her hand I look into her eyes.

"Juliette, I love you."

With what I hope is flair I pull a velvet box out of my jacket pocket. I open it up and take out the ring. She gasps, drops the reins as she covers her heart with her hand.

"I love being with you, living with you, doing things with you. When I imagine my future, you're who I'm with. You're who I want to have a family with, you're who I want to grow old with. My life is better with you; I'm a better man with you." I take a deep breath and look into her eyes. "Will you marry me?"

She bites her lip and sucks in some air.

My palms are sweaty as Juliette's hand starts to shake. I slip the ring on her finger.

"Oh, Nate," she gasps.

I look up at her face. A tear rolls down her cheek. For a split second, I wonder if she'll reject me. Then in a burst of emotion, she throws her arms around me.

"Yes, of course, I'll marry you. I love you."

Author's Notes

WAIT! IT'S NOT OVER. Next up is Hita's story. You'll get to see more of Juliette and Nate along with meeting some of the other princesses.

Writing this series has been an incredible experience. I've spent many enjoyable hours developing Nate's story. I hope that you have as much fun reading about him as I had creating him.

I'd like to give a special call out my wonderful beta readers who gave me great insight: Ann Quesinberry, Deb Kiger, and Margie Dean. Also, Eilish Byrne, for double-checking the accuracy of the Physical Therapy terminology.

For more on The Princesses, my blog, and a visual tour of the places Nate has visited, you can go to my website: http://www.anitaclaire.com.

Visit my Facebook page: – where I post interesting information, notices when a new book comes out, and give-a-ways.

Visit my blog, http://www.anitaclaire.com/blog where I have posted all the chapters I pulled when I consolidated from three books to one book.

As an indie writer, I live for my readers. If you enjoyed this book, please write a review, your opinion matters.

Other Books by Anita Claire

BOOKS IN "THE REUNION" series
Three contemporary romances stories that take place at a twenty-year high school reunion

Abby and Quinn
Kate and Noah
Harper and Liam

Books in "A Silicon Valley Prince" series
Three contemporary romance stories about adults in their 30's.

The Story of Jax and Payton
The Story of Brody and Ana
The Story of Flint and Lexi

Books in "The Princess of Silicon Valley" series
A collection of eight, coming of age, romance stories.

The Juliette Chronicles
Book 1 – Juliette
Book 2 – Nate
Book 3 – Hita

Best Friends Trilogy
Book 1 – Jennifer and Rocket
Book 2 – Isabelle
Book 3 – Kelly

Sisters from Another Mother
Book 1 – Olivia
Book 2– Meredith and Sam

Book 1 of The Princesses of Silicon Valley

SOMETIMES IT'S HARD *to choose*

Meet Juliette Cole, she's just arrived back to Silicon Valley after three heartbreaking months following her grad school love to London. Moving in with childhood friend turned blond bombshell, she gets introduced to Cassie's crazy over the top lifestyle. Taking a job at a Silicon Valley startup, she learns that work is more than hoodies and free gourmet food. Thankfully she has The Princesses, her close group of girlfriends from college, who all went as princesses to a Halloween party their freshman year.

They don't call San Jose- Man Jose for nothing. Juliette's heart is not lonely for long. Swimming before work, she sees a guy with the most amazing six pack get out of the pool. Now she has a new quest – to meet him. While playing soccer, she gets knocked out by an opposing player. The player's hot doctor brother helps her to the sidelines, then starts texting her. As things start heating up in Juliette's personal life, she now has two guys vying for her attention. Who will it be, sexy swimmer Zach or hot Dr. Nate?

Book 2 of The Princesses of Silicon Valley

SOME NICE GUYS WEREN'T *always so nice*

Nate's a guy who prides himself on his no commitment lifestyle. He's a master at zeroing in on the hottest woman for a quick and easy hookup, making a point of never spending the night. Until he runs into a woman that makes him want more than a one-night stand. After she blows his heart away he starts reevaluating his choices.

Now it's Nate's turn. Following Nate from high school through his twenties, we learn that this wonderful man has a lot of history that would surprise Juliette if she ever found out. Enjoy their story from Nate's point of view. Find out what happens next.

This is a stand-alone book, but much more fun if read along with the other Princess stories.

Book 3 of The Princess of Silicon Valley

SOME GIRLS JUST WANT *to have fun*

Hita's Indian mom is working overtime introducing her to the right sort of Indian man to marry. While Hita just wants to have fun, explore life, and meet some guy who will knock her socks off. Though single life in Silicon Valley is not as carefree as she'd hope for, and finding the right man is easier said than done. After a string of dating disasters, she finds out that maybe true love has been under her nose the whole time.

Of course, Hita has her band of college friends supporting her the whole way; dubbed The Princesses from their freshman year Halloween costumes.

This is a stand-alone book, but much more fun if read along with the other Princess stories.

Book 4 of The Princesses of Silicon Valley

***SOMETIMES OPPOSITES** don't just attract - they catch fire and ignite*

Jennifer is a middle school teacher with an eye for metrosexual men. Her last boyfriend had more shoes than her. Having no interest in tatted up, pierced, and rough looking Rocket she dances with him anyway since it's only a dance. Wild Rocket has come back from a binge of drinking, fighting, and sleeping around. Finally deciding to get serious, he falls for pretty Jennifer and the hot way she shakes her butt on the dance floor.

In a moment of weakness, Jennifer agrees to join Rocket on a visit to an art gallery where she learns that maybe the book is deeper than the cover and love can be found in the least obvious places.

Of course, Jennifer has her band of college friends supporting her the whole way; dubbed The Princesses from their freshman year Halloween costumes. Told in alternating POV.

This is a stand-alone book, but much more fun if read along with the other Princess stories.

Book 5 of The Princesses of Silicon Valley

***SOMETIMES GOOD THINGS** can come out of disasters*

Isabelle is frustrated. All her friends are finding love while she's stuck living at home, has a lousy job, and is caught in a dysfunctional cycle with her on again off again ex-boyfriend.

Expanding her circle, she joins her new friends for a fun weekend in the mountains that turn into a disaster. Though sometimes good things come out of disasters and maybe Isabelle's fortunes are changing.

Brother's Jordan and Jake are up in Tahoe to mountain bike and water ski. Helping out Isabelle turns into more of an adventure than they ever bargained for.

Of course, Isabelle has her band of college friends supporting her the whole way; dubbed The Princesses from their freshman year Halloween costumes.

This is a stand-alone book, but much more fun if read along with the other Princess stories.

Book 6 of The Princesses of Silicon Valley

SOMETIMES EVERYTHING *that you want is right in front of you*

Kelly has always been a wild child. She travels the world partying, competing in sports and hooking up – and not necessarily in that order. She's never had an interest in living in one place, having a steady boyfriend, or getting a job. Until she meets a guy who changes her mind about everything.

Of course, Kelly has her band of college friends that compel her to keep coming back to Silicon Valley; dubbed The Princesses from their freshman year Halloween costumes.

This is a stand-alone book, but much more fun if read along with the other Princess stories.

Book 7 of The Princesses of Silicon Valley

SOMETIMES YOU CAN'T *stop your heart from its desire*

Olivia is the complete package; beauty, brains, and money. More than that, she's the ultimate play-girl, since she's not afraid to reel the men in and keep them hooked. When her best friend introduces Olivia to her brother, she makes Oliva promise not to add him to her entourage of adoring men.

Down to earth Conner grew up on a farm and is now a solider. What happens when the ultimate city girl meets the country boy and realizes that these terms are only labels, and the label she likes best is authentic, and the man she can't resist is Conner. Can you fight against your heart's desire? Sometimes when your heart calls, promises must be broken.

Of course, Olivia has her band of college friends that compel her to keep coming back to Silicon Valley; dubbed The Princesses from their freshman year Halloween costumes.

This is a stand-alone book, but much more fun if read along with the other Princess stories.

Book 8 of The Princesses of Silicon Valley

SOMETIMES YOU CAN'T help falling in love

Meredith's mom dropped out of college when she got pregnant. There's no way Meredith will let any boy derail her dreams.

Sam is captivated by the pretty freshman with the big blue eyes. He's on a one-man mission to date her.

What happens when a shy stubborn country girl meets a warm charming city boy? Can Sam's persistence overcome Meredith's reluctance?

Of course, Meredith has her band of college friends dubbed The Princesses from their freshman year Halloween costumes. Meet the princesses in their freshman year of college and accompany them through their twenties as we follow Meredith and Sam's story.

This is a stand-alone book, but much more fun if read along with the other Princess stories.

A Silicon Valley Prince – Volume 1

PAYTON'S HECTIC SCHEDULE didn't include being ordered to show up at a customer's office after his computers are taken hostage.

Of course, Jax, the guy doing the ordering wasn't expecting his computer guy to be such a beauty.

Their first meeting doesn't get off too well as Jax blurts out, "Payton—the dude I've been texting back and forth with for the last two years—is really a girl?"

"Yeah, well, Jax, you look a lot different than what I pictured too." Except Payton finds Jax to be big, broad, and ruggedly handsome. Why do all the good-looking guys have to be such dicks? Payton wonders.

Jax can't stop watching this beauty fix his computers, while Payton's intrigued and repulsed all at the same time.

Afterward, Jax can't get Payton out of his mind. A couple of days later, wanting to see Payton again, Jax hatches a plan.

Nothing could have prepared Payton for the ride Jax would take her on. And she certainly wasn't prepared for where she'd wind up when the ride was over.

All good things must come to an end, right?

Except their ending was one Payton didn't see coming.

A Silicon Valley Prince – Volume 2

BRODY IS A BUSY MAN, he doesn't have time to date. He definitely doesn't have time for a girlfriend. Even so, he finds the pretty woman at the chiropractor's office appealing.

Ana, a wildlife biologist, social life has flatlined. She's surprised when the attractive man at her chiropractor's office jump starts her heart. After multiple unsuccessful attempts at trying to engage him, Ana tells him about one of her mountain lions getting poisoned.

Brody's interest is piqued. He decides to take a day off to help Ana find what affected her cat.

What Brody isn't prepared for is Ana. Can a man only focused on business realize that he's met the right woman? Can a woman with a bruised heart be open to the right man?

This is a stand-alone book, but much more fun if read along with the other Prince stories

A Silicon Valley Prince – Volume 3

FLINT HAS HAD A CRUSH on Lexi since he was fourteen. Being two years older, Lexi never really paid attention. Twenty years later... Lexi's personal life has come crashing down.

When Lexi's at her lowest, having a handsome man hitting on her sure feels good. It can't hurt to flirt back, right? Maybe he's the diversion she needs right now.

While Flint might have the chance to make his high school dreams come true.

This is a stand-alone book, but much more fun if read along with the other Prince stories

Enjoy an excerpt from

Hita

My phone rings three times. "Ya motha is calling, pick up da phone," an annoying woman with a New York accent whines out. It's a lot funnier ringtone when it's not seven thirty on Sunday morning.

"Hey, Mom," I answer with the cheeriest voice I can muster.

"Hita, it's about time you answered your phone. Your father and I are looking forward to coming out for your graduation. I've spoken to a couple of friends. Since we're traveling through California, they've invited us to tea."

"Mom, really, you had to wake me up to tell me this?"

"Hita, if you spend all day in bed, you won't do well on your finals."

"Mom, thanks for the advice," I groan out, trying to mask my sarcasm.

On some levels, I'm close to my mom. But when it comes to men and marriage, we're light years apart. My parents grew up in India and had an arranged marriage. Mom doesn't understand why I'm not cool with this for myself. Since I'm almost finished with grad school, Mom thinks it's time for me to get married. Right now she's in overdrive with matchmaking, trying to fix me up with Indians from the right sort of family.

This makes me feel conflicted by my ethnicity. I love my heritage, all the stories, the food, the colors, and celebrations; yet I have a big issue with the traditional roles my culture inflicts. I have no desire to be married off to some guy who expects me to do all the work around the house and then kowtow to his mother. Actually, when I'm ready to settle down I wouldn't mind marrying an Indian-America since he would get my family and we'd share a cultural heritage.

At twenty-three, the last thing on my mind is getting married and raising a family. I'm looking forward to getting a job, buying a car, and then having the time and money to do fun things, though I wouldn't mind finding a fun boyfriend who'd knock my socks off.

I met my last boyfriend at a gaming convention. Brandon's from Palo Alto, where I go to school. He was going to college up in Washington. Since we lived eight hundred miles apart, during the school year we'd meet up in our favorite games. It was a great way to date and much more fun than having lame conversations over Skype or FaceTime. Each time we'd meet up online, he'd pick me up in a different type of car, van, truck, motorcycle, or tank. We'd then fight bad guys together as we'd attempt to progress through a date. We spent time together in the real world when he came home for the summer and I worked at Google. But after spending almost four years dating long distance, I've decided that my next boyfriend will be local. I want more in my life than virtual hand holding and summertime sex.

As I head into the kitchen to make some coffee, I run into my roommate, Juliette. Our friendship was cemented our freshman year when seven of us went to the Halloween parties as princesses. I was Pocahontas—get it? I'm Indian. Juliette was Snow White since she has dark hair, brown eyes, and pale skin. Juliette spent her junior year in Spain, so I'm finishing grad school a year ahead of her.

"What's with your mom this morning?" Juliette asks.

"What else is with my mom?" Imitating Mom's sing-song accent, I mug, "Hita you need to find a husband. You're twenty-three years old. Men don't want to marry old women."

"At twenty-three, your mom thinks your time's almost expired?"

"Believe it or not, she's now trolling—who knows where—for the right kind of single Indian guys in Silicon Valley."

"There are plenty here to choose from though I can't see you with some off the boat, traditional Indian guy."

"I'm cool with going out with Indians and being Hindu, I can't see myself with a Christian. But I'm making my own choices, and when the time is right, I'm definitely marrying another American."

"I can't believe we're even talking about marriage. It seems like something that's so far away."

"I think it's because we're still in school."

"I don't know any guys who are even thinking about marriage. Most of the guys I know are too commitment-phobic to want a full-time girlfriend."

"All the guys I know think saying *hi* to a girl after a hook-up is bordering on commitment."

"I guess having a boyfriend makes me an outlier."

"True, what's with you and Stephen?"

"What do you mean?"

"Do you see a future?"

"I never really thought about that. I'm too busy trying to make it through school." She starts eating Cheerios out of the box. "Stephen is fun to be around," she adds. "He's got this quirky dry sense of humor that really cracks me up. Even more than that, I like having a boyfriend; I like being in a relationship...and the sex..." she teases, giving me a second to let my mind wander. She leans back and eats another Cheerio. "It sure beats some nasty hookup. But more than that? I don't know."

"Don't even talk to me about the sex," I groan out as I reach into the box and pull out a handful. "I wish I had a fun boyfriend, someone who lives close by and likes doing the same things as me."

"And the sex?" Juliette questions with a bit of a smirk.

"And the sex." I close my eyes and fantasize for a moment. "Yeah...and sex," I groan out.

"You need it bad, my friend,"

"You have no idea. But I have no interest in nasty hookups. What I'd like is to come home to something other than homework."

"Hey, what about me?"

"You're a great roommate and I love you, but, girlfriend, I don't swing that way. Anyway, I don't think Stephen would want me messing with his game."

"Oh don't fool yourself, girlfriend, every guy fantasizes about two women."

"That's never going to happen."

"That wasn't an offer. I told Stephen that if he wanted that kind of shit, he's dating the wrong girl."

"He asked you for a ménage à trois?"

"Not exactly, but we were watching Game of Thrones and his eyes lit up when they showed girl-on-girl. He actually replayed the scene three times."

"What did you say?"

"I told him if he wanted the kinky stuff, he should date Kelly. You should have seen his face. He was horrified. Kelly scares the shit out of him. He actually asked me if she's a guy in drag."

"She looks like a woman."

"I think he was talking about how she behaves. Anyway, why don't you date the guys your mom is busy dredging up? I'm sure one of them has to be cool."

"Any guy who lets his mom find a date for him has to be either too traditional or totally pathetic. Anyway, Indians don't have a dating culture. Indian moms spend a lot of time interviewing families to find prospective partners from their caste for their kids. The guy's family invites the girl's family to tea. If you're both interested in meeting again, it's three dates and you're engaged."

"You mean three figurative dates."

"NO. If you see the guy three times, the moms are looking for auspicious dates for the wedding."

"I can see why that would be a problem."

As I labor away on creating a kernel patch, my homework assignment, Skype goes off. I'm relieved, my brain was going nuts trying to get this sequence right. A picture of my childhood friend Savi comes up. We're both from Chicago. Our families are really close. We went to the same high school, attended the same Hindi class, and took Indian dance together.

"Hita, how goes it?"

"I'm trying to get this assignment done. I have so much to do before I graduate."

"Have you figured out what you're doing after graduation?"

"Actually, I'm interviewing at Apple tomorrow."

"You're not coming home?"

"To Chicago? Weren't you thinking of coming out here?"

"No, I think I'll live with my parents this summer. I'm still on the fence. I need to decide if I want to work before starting my Ph.D."

"Won't living at your parents be a little...stifling?"

"Of course it will be. But you know how hot Chicago summers are, we have the pool in the backyard and my grandparents aren't staying there this summer...so it won't be as bad."

"But what about guys?"

"If I had a boyfriend it would be terrible. You know how my parents are."

"But your mom? Is she starting to talk about...teas?"

"There's no way in hell I'm going to have an arranged marriage. My mom might be persistent, but I'm even more stubborn. Anyway, I don't date Indian guys. What about you?"

"I'm not dating anyone either."

"No, I mean your mom. Is she pushing for an Indian guy?"

"My mom's always pushing something. I live two thousand miles away. It's hard to be a matchmaker from a distance."

"But your parents are coming out for your graduation?"

"Well, yeah."

"I bet your mom is working overtime to set up some 'teas' with the right sort of families."

"Having tea at someone's house sounds so innocuous."

"It would be if our moms weren't busy using them to parade us in front of single, eligible, Indian men and their mom's."

"I might not be doing well finding a guy on my own, but my mother choosing a guy for me, now that would be a complete disaster."

"I'm American, I'll choose my own man, and live my own life. I know my mom would hate to hear this, but I'm never going to date an Indian. It's Americans all the way for me. Anyway, good luck with your interview," she confides before we both sign off.

* * * *

AWARE, I SIT ON A BLACK leather and chrome modern chair in the austere white four-story lobby, my nerves are amped up to the point where it feels like I've had five cups of coffee, not the one cup I drank.

"Hita Chamarthi?" a man calls out.,

With a deep breath, I give what I hope is a warm smile and extend my hand to an Asian guy in his late thirties. He bends his head slightly in response.

"Chéng-gong Chan," he mumbles.

Repeating his name multiple times in my head, I follow him through a labyrinth of halls into a white minimalist conference room. He sits down across from me. With a perfunctory smile, he looks at my résumé, scanning it up and down. "I see you are about to graduate with a Masters in Computational & Mathematical Engineering," he finally murmurs.

I'm not sure if this statement requires a response as he continues to read my résumé. "You've spent the last few summers working at Google, developing in Pig for a Hadoop system," he states out loud. I'm still unsure if this statement requires any response as he has yet to give me eye contact.

"We're looking for people to work on our big data solutions," he imparts as if this provides clarity. I'm still wondering if there is a question or if I should be verbally agreeing with his obvious statement. My mind wanders, I wonder what kind of technical questions he's going to ask. I've heard lots of stories about Silicon Valley job interviews. The current rage is to ask programming questions that can be completed in less than twenty minutes.

Lucky for me, Chéng-gong is going analytical. Being Chinese, I know he's memorized every definition and programming term he uses and will test me against his knowledge. My parents pushed me to memorize, a skill my American friends consider a waste of time since it's so easy to look everything up, but it comes in handy when I'm being tested by other Asians.

After almost forty-five minutes of what feels like a technical game of Jeopardy, his iPhone beeps. "My turn is over," he politely informs me. Slightly bowing, he gets up and leaves. I'm left alone in the room. Should I pull my Samsung phone out and start reading? Since this is Apple, I'm afraid if I'm caught using it they might construe me as sacrilegious.

The next three interviewers each give me a problem that I need to program. I thank my lucky stars I spent the last few weeks cramming from the book *Cracking the Coding Interview,* since all of the questions are right out of it. At lunch time, three of my interviewers take me to Café Macs. Everything is decorated minimalist with no colors, a big visual departure from Google which is decorated in their four primary colors. We sit under a large live oak, in the green space between all the buildings. Everyone is grumbling since they just raised the prices.

By my seventh interview of the day, I have no idea what products this group is working on or anything else about engineering since they're so paranoid. The hiring manager wouldn't even tell me how many people work for him. It must be because Steve Jobs stole most of his ideas from other companies, and he didn't want grad students to do that to him.

At the end of the day, I feel wrung out and exhausted. I've already decided that I'm not interested in working at Apple. They have twice the employees as Google. I want to work at someplace smaller.

The next week I interview at a well-funded start-up that's located in San Francisco. I have a number of friends from school who now live there. Even though some of the Silicon Valley companies are building offices in San Francisco, most of my friends commute down to Silicon Valley. The choice is to live for the week or to live for the weekend. If I get a job in San Francisco then I get the best of both worlds, a short commute and hip city living.

From the train, I walk to their offices located in a trendy refurbished warehouse. After waiting in their urban cool lobby, a hipster looking guy comes out to get me. The interviews proceed similarly to the ones at Apple. Again, they all ask me to program using samples from, *Cracking the Coding Interview*. Which makes me wonder if everyone is studying from the same book, how can they figure what anyone knows?

All the guys I meet tell me they're developers, but they dress rather hip and brag about the perks, though besides free food, I wonder how they have time to use any of them. One of the guys comes in carrying his messenger bag. Back in college, all the engineers used backpacks; it was the business guys who used messenger bags. I'm wondering how solid these guys are, or if they're just Brogrammers – a bunch of former college frat guys and athlete code monkeys who only know how to develop apps and front-end applications? I'm an engineer, I want to use math to solve the hard problems.

When I get in front of one of the senior managers, I ask him how much funding they have. I quickly calculate that with forty employees and a fancy facility they will run out of money by the end of the year.

Then the manager tells me they are behind on their deliverables, and now need to hire people who have the skills to handle big data. This makes me wonder if I'm the only person in this building that knows they're in trouble.

At school, the Venture Capitalists (VC)—the guys who finance new companies—have been swirling around the engineering building. It's always a great way to grab some free food. But I'm not yet interested in starting my own company. I'd like to work for someone else for a few years.

My professors have brought in some of their former students to judge and discuss our projects. The alumni use these opportunities to pitch their company to prospective employees. A few of the new companies actually look interesting. One of the speakers, Flint, is a guy I worked with my first summer at Google. He remembers me and asks for my résumé. His company is three years old with over a hundred employees, a product with customers, and revenue.

When I go for the interview, their offices are in a new building that's been decorated simply, with brightly painted walls, and hallways covered in whiteboards. My potential co-workers seem to be smart, relatively normal, and technically competent. The company has a really young vibe since everyone appears to be under thirty. Even better, they're still pre-IPO, so there's a potential financial upside that's more than my salary. This company feels like a winner.

Getting back to graduate housing, Juliette's in the living room hanging with her boyfriend Stephen. I liked her college boyfriend Chris, a lot better. Stephen has this arrogant attitude like he's lived so much more than we have, even though he's only a year older. Juliette leaves Stephen in the living room and follows me into the kitchen.

"How'd your interview go?"

"One more interview, one more day of mind-numbing questions," I answer after grabbing a drink out of the refrigerator. "I don't know how they can figure out if I'll be a good engineer based on what they ask me."

"What questions did they ask?"

As I wait for the microwave to beep, I throw out the questions as Juliette and I discuss potential answers.

"I wonder what answers they were really looking for?"

"Have you thought about which company you want to work at?"

"This last one's the best. They're solving the hard problems; it seems like they have their act together when it comes to managing their money, and I didn't run into any brogrammers or preeners."

Chapter 3 – Graduation

The job offer from Flint's company comes in. To celebrate, Jennifer, a college friend who went to the Halloween parties as Mulan and I head to Nola, a fun, loud, New Orleans themed restaurant.

"I see *Mr. Big Love* is joining us," Jennifer quips as Meredith my college roommate shows up with her longtime boyfriend, Sam.

Juliette shows up with Stephen. "Of course he's going to order something unique and pretentious that no one has ever heard of," Meredith groans under her breath.

"I wonder if Juliette can't see his annoying characteristics because he's so handsome," Jennifer comments.

We order margaritas and a bunch of appetizers, laughing and joking and generally enjoying ourselves. I drink too much as everyone toasts to my future success. "I better enjoy tonight's fun since I'm headed into the storm of my last finals week ever."

"Here's to the last finals ever," Juliette toasts as she lifts her glass into the air.

"You my friend still have another year," I can't help but to remind her.

My good cheer is short-lived. The next day my professor gives us a twenty-four-hour test. That is a take-home test that needs to be turned in within twenty-four hours after receiving it, which makes it sound easy. The thing is, the questions are so difficult it takes twenty-four hours to answer them all. I hate pulling all-nighters. By about three in the morning, I'm starting to hallucinate, I'm getting to the point where I don't care what the answers are.

After finals, I sleep for twenty-four hours solid; waking up in time for my parents to show up for graduation. Juliette and I make dinner for my parents the night they arrive.

"Hita, it is such a tragedy that Google didn't offer you a job. I hear they're the best place to work," mom bemoans as we sit down to eat.

With my best consolatory face, I shake my head and give Juliette the eye since she knows Google was one of the job offers I turned down.

After my parents head back to their hotel, Juliette pulls out the margaritas. Meredith and Jennifer show up. They both scarf down all the leftovers.

"I thought it was going to be fun to take a couple of weeks off and travel down the coast with my parents, but my mom is using it as an opportunity to introduce me to all these Indian guys. I feel like I'm headed to the parade of losers."

"Why don't you look at it positively and date some of the guys your mom wants to fix you up with?" Meredith naively responds.

"These are Indians we're talking about. It's not like I can go out with some guy and if I don't like him, move on to the next one. If I start casually dating real Indian guys, I'll quickly get a bad reputation. I'm too loyal of a daughter to dishonor my parents like that."

"Vihaan dated Claudia. Now he's dating Suzanne," Jennifer chimes in.

"I bet he's not introducing those women to his family and friends of his family. He's keeping those relationships on the down low. Real Indian guys might casually date Americans, and some of them even marry Americans. But dating is frowned upon. That's the problem I have with my mom's fix-ups. The guy might be nice, but I'm not ready to make this big of a decision after one family dinner. If I say yes to a date, the families will start planning the wedding."

"I'm glad I'm not Indian. Chris and I didn't work out," Juliette bemoans.

"Though, he was hot," I respond.

"My favorite part of dating him was his water polo matches."

"The best part of you dating him was joining you at those water polo matches," Jennifer says as she raises her glass to cheer.

"Water polo players are hot," Meredith adds.

"And speedos are the best uniform ever."

• • • •

THE DAY AFTER I GRADUATE, Savi Skypes me. "CONGRATULATIONS!" she screams into her microphone.

"Wow, you almost blew my ear off with that one."

"How does it feel to be done with grad school?"

"It hasn't yet hit. How's living at home?"

"Ali and I are heading to Chicago this weekend to party with Lauren, you know, she has an apartment in the city."

"Your mom isn't trying to meddle?"

"Not yet, maybe I've been worried about nothing. How about you? Are you looking forward to your trip down the coast with your parents?"

"You're luckier than me. I think my mom has already scheduled some teas."

"What are you going to do?"

"What choice do I have? I'll tell her I'm not going out with those guys, but it's easier to play along. I figure they'll go home in a couple of weeks and I can go back to my normal life."

"Good plan, I agree. I have no interest in the guy's my mom chooses. They're always so dorky. I'd only consider dating another Indian if he was normal, you know, cool, American. Why is it that Indian guys are either dorky or players? Aren't there any normal ones out there?"

"Most of the Indian guys here are H-1B."

"Like that would ever happen."

"I've noticed you have a thing for the White boys."

"True, but it would make life easier if I could meet a nice American-born Indian, another Hindu. They would understand my family dynamics."

I nod in agreement.

• • • •

A FEW HOURS LATER, my parents show up. They help me store my stuff for the next few weeks in Juliette's parents' garage. Then we head to a friend of my mom's cousins in Cupertino for tea. I bet this friend is from our caste and has a single son in his twenties.

"I'm finding my own man," I explain to mom one more time as we drive to these strangers home.

"Hita, you play those computer games. Nothing's going to come of that," mom dismisses my comment with her sweet, sing-song voice.

At the house we go to, both parents answer the door. The mom is wearing a deep green silk sari and lots of gold jewelry. After entering their home, they make a point of pausing in front of their expensive gold shrine to Ganesh, which takes up most of the dining room. Then we're ushered into their living room. The mother serves us chaat tea, fancy nuts, and biscuits on her best china. While we're seated on their modern leather furniture, I note that it's a nice house, all decorated with an Indian flare that includes oriental rugs, bright colors, and elaborately carved accessories.

Everyone is polite and friendly as the parents talk and the son checks me out. At five ten, I'm tall. Mom did a poor job with research; the son comes to my shoulder. I plaster a polite smile on my face knowing I'll never date him. His lack of height doesn't stop my mom. She pushes the conversation, lightly bragging about my graduation and new job. His mom takes it in stride as she waits to brag about her son's education and his job.

Looking at the mother, I realize that if I get involved with an Indian guy and his parents live locally, they'll be in my business more than my mom has ever been. Even worse, if his parents live in India they will come for a visit and stay for five months. I grew up watching my paternal grandmother run my mother ragged when she came for her visits.

My mind reels. I've been so busy with school, I've never really considered what it would be like to date in the real world, now I'm wondering what my next chapter will bring.

My mother's relentless pursuit of a husband for me, overhangs our trip. We stop for *tea* at a number of Indian homes on our way up and down the coast. It's almost a relief when I see my parents off upon our return to Silicon Valley.

When I get back I Skype with Savi, she lets me bitch about my mom. Savi and I understand each other well since she also has spent her lifetime bridging the American and Indian worlds.

• • • •

ARRIVING BACK FROM my trip, I stay with Juliette at her parents' house for a few days, until I can get into my apartment. Sitting on a lounge chair soaking up the rays while my feet casually dip into their pool, the doorbell rings. I throw on my T-shirt and answer the door. Since I assume it's going to be a package, I'm surprised when it's Juliette's friend, Gray.

"You're Juliette's roommate, right?"

"We've met a couple of times, I'm Hita."

"Is Juliette home?"

"She started her summer internship this week. I'm staying here for a few days. You know, transitioning between apartments."

"I start my summer internship on Monday. I didn't realize Juliette wasn't going to be around. Are you hanging out by the pool?" he asks as he looks me up and down.

"If you don't have plans you can join me."

"Sure, give me ten minutes. I'll go home and get my trunks."

"Don't ring the bell when you come back, let yourself in through the back gate."

I watch him jog down the path. I head back to my lounge chair and continue with my book. Hanging out with Gray should be fun. I was getting kind of bored being by myself. About ten minutes later, I feel a shadow move over me.

"That was quick," I exclaim as I look up from my book. Gray's wearing sunglasses and a baseball cap, but I can tell he's checking me out. I hold up a bag of Doritos. "Want some?"

He shakes his head as he plops down on the lounge chair next to mine. "What are you reading?" I pass my tablet to him. He reads a passage. "A Game of Thrones? Have you watched the shows?"

"I've been too busy with school. A friend said I would enjoy the shows a lot more if I read the books first."

"This is a great series. You wouldn't believe what..."

I quickly cover my ears and close my eyes.

"Don't tell me." I open one eye to look at him.

"Have you gotten to the place where...?"

I cover my ears and close my eyes again.

"Nanananana," I start chanting. "No, don't spoil it."

With one eye open, I find Gray has moved close.

"When Lord Eddard is...." he calls out as soon as he notices I've pulled my hands off my ears.

I jump up and cover that sassy mouth with my hand.

"Don't spoil it." He licks my hand. "Ewe, that was disgusting," I pull my hand away. "Will you behave yourself?"

His smile is devious as he leans in to pull a couple of chips out of the bag and munches them loudly.

"Are you hot? Want to take a dip?"

"Only if you promise not to give anything away."

With a Cheshire grin, he shrugs. Casually he pulls off his T-shirt. Damn, I had no idea he had such a nice chest...and abs...and... As I force my eyes up, I see a slight smile on his face; he's caught me checking him out. Damn, I have to say, one of my favorite things is when a guy has a cute, above average face, that's pleasant and approachable but doesn't look too much like a model...and then reveals a killer body hiding beneath his clothes. Oh man, I needed to jump in the pool to cool down.

"First one wet wins," I yell.

I jump into the pool. The cool water tingles my skin. Gray and I spend the next couple of hours playing, first pool volleyball, then we use noodles to see who can race across the pool the fastest. Finally, we have a contest to see who can make the biggest splash. This morning reminds me of when I was ten. Back then I'd play in the pool for hours.

Gray looks even better wet than he does dry. Damn, why am I even going there? I've been so busy with school these last few weeks I haven't had time to think about men. But now...it's like my brain is in overdrive.

With our lips turning blue, we both lie on the deck allowing the warmth from the concrete to fill our bones.

"I'm starving," Gray groans out.

"I'd feel funny raiding Juliette's parents' kitchen."

"We can grab something at Armadillo Willies."

"I'm a vegetarian."

"They have vegetarian burgers."

"Okay." I stand up, pull my shorts and T-shirt over my bikini, and run a brush through my hair. Now I know why Gray and Juliette are so close; he's fun and easy to hang out with. I watch him throw his T-shirt back on. Hita, keep your mind out of the gutter. An X-rated video with Gray as the lead flashes past my eyes.

When we return from burgers and drinks, I yawn. "I think I'm ready for a siesta." I pull off my T-shirt and shorts and settle into the lounge chair. Damn, my fingers itch to touch Gray. But I keep reminding myself he's Juliette's good friend. Would kissing him break some kind of girl code? Anyway, he's taking off in a couple of days. I'm not doing another long-distance relationship.

Gray maneuvers the umbrella so it's covering my lounge chair. "A siesta would be nice," he comments as he pulls off his T-shirt.

Am I particularly horny, or is his bare torso that amazing? My over stimulated libido wants to touch all those rippling muscles tightly packed under his beautiful golden skin.

I stretch out, feeling like a well-fed cat as I will myself to cool down. Gray sits down next to me and gives me a sexy smile. Then he runs the back of his fingers down my arm. It sends a tingle down the back of my neck as I hear myself gasp. His smile turns intense as he watches my face while moving even closer. I'm surprised by this bold move. Does he know what I'm thinking? Are our thoughts running in the same direction?

His breathing intensifies, I can tell he wants to kiss me, and I want to kiss him too. The sound of the water makes me feel like we're in our own private oasis. My fingers glide up his beautifully toned arm as I enjoy the ridges of his muscles.

My eyes focus on his lips. They look nice and inviting. We each move slowly toward each other, like magnets. Our lips meet. It's been way too long between kisses. I take the lead and lightly kiss him. His lips feel soft and firm. It's the first kiss I've had since Brandon and I broke up last December. Gray leans in a little farther, as we kiss again in full earnestness.

The smell of chlorine and sunscreen oozes through his pores. I wrap my arm around his shoulder; my hand lays flat on his warm back. Our kiss gets deeper as our tongues meet. He tastes of the chocolate chip cookie we shared. As our tongues dance, I can feel a sexual energy awaken inside me as it rolls down my core. He positions himself over me as he continues our kiss. I run my hand down his well-developed chest; lust fills every one of my pores as our kiss heats up. He maneuvers the lounge chair so it's flat. I bark out a laugh as it drops down, he smiles wide and leans in to kiss me again.

His hands run along my body leaving a trail of shimmering excitement in their path. I gasp as all reason escapes me and his lips leave mine. He runs a trail of kisses to my ear, I giggle from the sensation along my jaw. He continues to kiss me. His lips trail down my neck. My head rolls as I arch my back. Desire fills me like a drug. His hands are on my breasts as his tongue licks my nipple. His breath tingles, I shiver, sit up, and cup his head. He sucks my nipple into his mouth. I squeal. Our eyes connect.

"Don't stop, please, don't stop," I plead.

He smiles. I lean back and close my eyes. All control has left me as I yearn for more. His amazing lips and tongue move farther down. I spread my legs. I want satisfaction; I crave that feeling, the one you get when you lose yourself to an orgasm. He rains gentle kisses down my stomach. My diaphragm tightens. I gasp loudly from pleasure. His clever fingers run up my inner thigh, a light touch that's almost a tickle. He reaches my core, moves my bikini bottoms out of the way, and probes my folds. I ride his hand. He's surprisingly skilled, or was Brandon clumsy? Whatever, his touch feels good, I crave more.

"Don't stop," I gasp loudly.

He chuckles as he continues to probe and play with me as I buck into him. The tingles move into spasms as an orgasm starts to form.

Gray stops touching me.

"No, I'm almost there," I gasp out.

"Let me join you," his voice is soft as he pleads.

I nod. A condom rips. Where did he keep that? Slowly I open my eyes, his intense face floats over me. I cup his head and then run my fingers through his hair as our lips meet. Instinctively, I wrap my legs around his hips. My orgasm is so close, I crave the release. I want more friction. His fingers find my clit, rubbing it in the way that brings satisfaction. As the surge intensifies I gasp from contact. He runs his dick along my folds, finding its way inside of me.

Quickly he plunges into me. I gasp from the pain of his size and the shock of the fast, hard movement. He rocks in and out. The friction feels heavenly as my orgasm picks up and continues to peak. My breath is heavy as I gasp and the wooden chaise creaks in time with his rhythm.

Sensations build, his pace increases, my body explodes. Vibrations run through my central nervous system. Gray gasps, his thrusts slow but get deeper. My legs shimmy and shake as a fountain of tingles run up my core and bursts down my legs and arms. A deep buzzing feeling forms then explodes through the top of my head. I'm still gasping when he stops rocking. I hold onto him tightly as I explode. I had no idea an orgasm could burst, shatter and buzz like this. I kiss his face, neck, and shoulder. We're both damp from sex.

"Hita, I need some air," he gasps into my ear.

"Sorry," self-consciously I utter as I release my grasp. The cool air flows over my still shaking body. Our eyes connect, he smiles. "That was amazing," I manage to say.

He nods, leans in, and softly kisses my cheek.

"It was for me too. But I need to go."

I close my eyes and nod enjoying the bliss that's filling my soul. I have no idea where he's going. I'm so overwhelmed by sensations I don't have the presence of mind to ask. He gets up, adjust the umbrella. The shade covers my limbs. Gray trails a finger down my side. His touch makes me jump and shiver. I raise my arms and stretch out long and lean like a cat as sleep takes me under.

• • • •

"HITA," MOM'S VOICE makes me jump. "Is this how a good Indian girl behaves?" she scolds.

Surprised, I suddenly find myself awake. Mom of course, is back in Chicago; Gray is gone, and I'm naked, in Juliette's backyard. Shit, what if someone had come home? In haste I wrap myself in one of the big beach towels, grab my clothes and run into the house where I head directly to the shower.

As the water runs over my skin, the day plays out. Did I imagine this afternoon? Where did Gray go? I don't even have his number, and what do I say to Juliette? Do I tell her he came over? Do I tell her we had sex? The water runs over my still sensitive skin as my emotions run from perplexed to totally confused.

My soon-to-be roommate is Kristi. Conveniently for me, her soon-to-be former roommate is in the process of moving in with her boyfriend. Even better, Kristi's apartment is only a couple of miles from my new job.

Kristi lived on my floor freshman year. She has light brown shoulder length hair, caramel colored eyes, and a slim build. She was a computer science major; I still can't figure out how she put up with all the brogrammers. She's now developing iOS apps at some company that's doing some kind of disruptive technology. Though I have no idea what it is since she's under a non-disclosure and can't discuss anything.

Since I haven't yet bought a car, I ride my bike to the office. No one in my group shows up before ten, while they all stay until well into the evening. Our office reminds me of the dorms, though the food is better. Which makes it easy to fall into the trap of staying late to eat dinner at work. When I finally get home I'm not ready for bed. Instead, I stay awake all hours as I meet up online with friends to play games.

At work, I sit next to Chris and Avery. It's kind of hard to believe that they've only known each other since joining this company last year. They're like twins separated at birth. They're always talking about sports. When it comes to programming, Avery has an amazing memory and can write a lot of code, while Chris is slower but much more accurate. He also is better at debugging all the mistakes everyone else makes. He likes to wear headphones when he works, then munches really loudly on chips. I think I'll purchase headphones, just to cancel out Chris's chewing noises.

Growing up, we had a ping pong table in our basement. My brother and I used to have these crazy tournaments. I've started taking a mid-afternoon break to play ping pong against some of the other engineers. Two Chinese guys who are regulars, play well, though everyone else plays a lot better than me. The ping pong guys are nice enough, using me as their easy warm up. I figure if I keep it up I'll improve. I hope that making my afternoon break ping pong instead of dessert will save me from putting on the dreaded fifteen.

My third week of work, Sid, our engineering VP, holds an all-hands meeting taking over the cafeteria. There are probably seventy people in the room. He introduces all the new employees, having each of us stand up while everyone politely claps. Looking around the room, I only see three other women. A third of the men are Indian, another third are Asian, and the remaining third are White. The only Black guy is our Chief Legal Counsel, who gives us a talk at the beginning of the meeting on copyright, copyleft, and freeware, detailing what code we can use.

Stopping at the dessert bar after the meeting, I debate if I should get something. Colin, a tall, lean, nice looking guy with an olive complexion and a hint of blond in his dark hair joins me.

"Hey Hita, will you be at the tables at four?"

"Yes."

"Sweet, I'll see you then."

Cool, the ping pong guys actually want me to show up. Feeling happy, I decide against a dessert. Instead, I head to the table set up with company swag—all the company merchandise. They actually have good quality bike helmets with our company logo emblazoned into the plastic. This is thrilling since my helmet is ancient and I was thinking I should be buying a new one, too bad they don't have good quality headphones. As I check helmet sizes, a woman who looks about my age comes over and introduces herself.

"Hey, you're new here? I'm Kami."

"Oh, hi, I'm Hita. I just started working in the Trend Analysis group."

The other young woman engineer joins Kami. "I'm Caroline" she introduces herself as she extends her hand for me to shake. "Kami and I work in the Dashboard group." Caroline looks around at all the men.

"There's only a few women in Engineering. We need to stick together. You should join us for lunch or dinner."

"That would be nice."

I'm used to working with guys, but it's nice to break with all the testosterone and meet up with women. I've been eating lunch with three men in our group; Mark, Avery, and Chris. I've yet to figure out if they can talk about anything besides baseball statistics. At home, I stream the movie *Money Ball*, with the hope it will give me enough background information to follow their conversations.

The day after the engineering meeting, I get an e-mail from Kami inviting me to join her and Carolyn. I figure I can eat lunch with the guys on my team and save dinner for the other women in engineering.

• • • •

SINCE JULIETTE IS LIVING at home this summer, we wind up spending a lot of time on our weekends by her pool. Even better, her parents' refrigerator is always full, which saves me from having to grocery shop. As we start talking about the guys where we each work, her mom joins us.

"Any recommendations about dating guys you meet at work?" Juliette asks her mom.

"Tread lightly," her mom replies.

"You worked with Dad, that's how you two met."

"I knew your dad for three years before we started dating."

"I had no idea," Juliette exclaims. "You liked dad for three years before you two started dating?"

"No, I knew your father for three years. That's what's nice about meeting a guy at work. You have a long time to get to know the man. I was a project manager. We both were sent to Munich, Germany on a project with Siemens. It was the two of us Americans. All the Germans left the office by six to go home and have dinner with their families.

Three weeks of eating dinner together and spending the weekends sightseeing…brought us together and changed our point of view."

"Then I take it you don't see any problems with co-workers dating?" I state.

"I wouldn't recommend using work as your hook-up pool. Behaviors outside of work can easily be talked about at work and ruin your credibility. Also, if you start dating your boss, or your boss's boss, you'll either need to move jobs so you report to someone outside of your boyfriend's chain of command, or you'll need to leave the company. A manager will need to report a relationship with an underling to HR and legal. There are a number of high profile executives who've lost their job for dating people who work for them and didn't report the relationship. The last thing you want is to have your name associated with a scandal. No one will hire you, you'll become too high risk."

"Dating an executive will get you fired?" Juliette asks in surprise.

"Typically, it's not the dating that ever gets anyone fired. It's the breakup that gets people. It opens companies up to too many legal issues. Boards and VC's think if an executive is dating an underling, they're not thinking strategically."

"But what about co-workers?" I ask.

"No one cares if you keep it low profile and out of the office. Again, it's the breakup that causes problems. Juliette's dad and I worked in different buildings and reported to different VPs. When we got back to the states and started dating, we kept our relationship out of work. When Juliette's dad asked me to marry him, a lot of people didn't even know we were dating. Everyone was very supportive. Companies don't mind stable relationships. What they don't like is drama."

That night I think about what Juliette's mom said. I figure I'll play it cool and see if any of the guys at work stand out. Which gives me an idea. Once on my computer, I navigate to an Indian dating site. As I fill out the online form, I realize that the problem I have is I know how Indian guys think. It's almost the opposite of American guys. On the first or second date, they'll ask me if I plan on getting married. If I tell them I'm only twenty-three and want to date, they'll consider me a "bad" girl. We'll date, but they won't introduce me to their family. If I tell them yes, I want to get married, they'll have me meet their family and friends on the next date, and we'll be on the fast track to a wedding. This depresses me. As I stare at the form, I realize I want to be like Meredith and Juliette. I want a long term boyfriend and no pressure to marry. Closing down the dating site's window, I figure if I haven't found someone by the time I turn thirty, I'll get back on the site and find myself a husband.

I lean back in my chair looking up at the ceiling. I feel confused and perplexed about Gray. I figured with his job this summer in New York and going to school in Berkeley, he wasn't up for a girlfriend. But I thought we shared something, that we had a connection. It felt like something more than just an afternoon hookup. Then again, I never did tell Juliette. What was I going to say?

My mind then moves to Brandon. It feels like ages since we broke up. In December, it will be a year. I never told my parents about him, they would have freaked out. Unfortunately, Brandon was a lot more fun when we were dating long distance via computer games than when he lived in town. After he graduated and moved back to Palo Alto, our relationship fell apart. Mostly it was because I was busy studying nights and weekends. Brandon wanted more of my time than I could give. Now that I'm working, I wonder if it will be easier to have time for a boyfriend.